Wild Horses
And Other Short Stories

Joyce Keveren

Copyright © 2021 by Joyce Keveren

All rights reserved. No part of this publication may be reproduced, distributed, or transmitted in any form or by any means, including photocopying, recording, or other electronic or mechanical methods, without the prior written permission of the publisher, except in the case brief quotations embodied in critical reviews and other noncommercial uses permitted by copyright law.

ISBN: 978-1-63945-063-3 (Paperback)
        978-1-63945-064-0 (E-book)

The views expressed in this book are solely those of the author and do not necessarily reflect the views of the publisher, and the publisher hereby disclaims any responsibility for them.

Writers' Branding
1800-608-6550
www.writersbranding.com
orders@writersbranding.com

WILD HORSES

*E*very generation thinks they invented sex. I know mine did, or at least Ramon and I thought so, but that was a long time ago.

Still, I think of Ramon. We first met when we were in third grade. He had a round happy face and he was always smiling and that showed off the two dimples in his fat cheeks. He had dark brown curly hair and big chocolate colored eyes that were shiny. My mom even admitted that she always wanted to hug him, maybe even adopt him. I knew his family would not like that. I would have liked it though.

His family lived in a small house on the edge of a large sugar beet field north of town. My parents and I lived in a three-room apartment over the grocery store down on Main Street.

The town, which had around 2500 people, was called Buffalo Gap. It huddled on the western slope of the Big Horn Mountains in west central Wyoming. It was a nice little town with a brand-new state of the art movie theatre.

Ramon and I went to the Saturday matinee at that fancy new theatre every week. We started to wait for each other and go in together. We didn't talk about it; we just did it. At school, we would exchange shy glances and we would say hi in passing. Once in a while, we would sit on the bench together where the country kids like Ramon would wait for the bus and talk about the last movie we had seen.

Then in fourth grade, when we were ten, two brothers moved into town and were put in our class. Both of them were bullies, or bullies-in -training and they chose me to torment just like a pack of hyenas choose their prey: I was smaller than most of the other kids and I was shy.

That winter was so cold the school flooded an empty field to make an ice-skating rink and everyone who had skates skated at recess and noon hour. I finally got skates that year at Christmas and I tried them out on the edge of a small pond in the park near our apartment. The ice there was lumpy and rough and I fell often, but it was practice for me every day during Christmas break.

When school started again, the Bully Brothers watched me on the ice in my new skates and began to point and yell and dive bomb me on their skates until it worked and I fell down which brought on everyone looking and laughing.

Ramon skated out to me and helped me up, saying, "Get away from her," to the brothers. "Now," he whispered in my ear, "get out there and SKATE. You told me you practiced. Go do it. Show them all."

I looked up at him. He was smiling at me and I got up and did it. I skated away from Ramon and around that rink like I had been doing it forever.

Two big changes came about that day. One, those brothers stopped bothering me; they not only left me alone, they seemed afraid of me. Ramon and I didn't fully understand the other big change until much later, but from then on, Ramon tried to take care of me and I tried to take care of him. We began to trust each other and it felt good and comfortable. Neither one of us, at ten, had any idea how deep the connection between us was.

Later, in about seventh or eighth grade, Ramon started asking me to the school dances and everyone pretty much shut up about our skin colors and backgrounds or whatever else was bothering them and they all finally just understood we were together whether they liked it or not.

Ramon's family was from Mexico. They came north to Buffalo Gap to work in the sugar beet fields. Years back, Ramon told me, before any of the kids were born, his mom and dad would go back home to Sonora every fall after the harvest and return again the next spring. The owner of the farm eventually gave Ramon's father a year-round job when he discovered that Arturo was good with horses and knew cattle too because he had worked on a large cattle ranch in Sonora.

He started breaking the horses to ride too and he taught Ramon his techniques so Ramon worked part time when he turned twelve. Ramon loved working with the horses. His father's method was slow and gentle and required great patience and a lot of time. Ramon learned it well, and he loved helping to break the young horses, but he especially loved to help drive the cattle up to the BLM grazing lease on the top of the mountain in May when school let out.

I liked Ramon's dad; he was always kind to me even though he liked to tease me and Ramon would translate for him. Ramon's mother was very shy and she thought her English wasn't good, so we rarely spoke, but she fed me and smiled.

I think that she was also a bit jealous because it looked to me like Ramon, who was her first born, was also her favorite. And of course, she wanted her handsome son to marry a good Catholic girl, not me. My alcoholic father was an avowed atheist and my mother was an evangelical, fundamentalist, pious church going lady who hated Catholics for no apparent reason I could discern other than she learned it from her English Protestant relatives, all of whom must have forgotten they got their religion, not from God, but from a fat, corrupt old king who only wanted a divorce and didn't give one damn about religion. Neither one of my parents were shy about telling anyone their beliefs or lack of them either.

"Jesus, Mary and Joseph," Ramon said with a grin, "such heresy."

Ramon and I had fun together. He had a wicked sense of humor. He could speak three languages and was learning a fourth. Spanish was his first language and he had learned Yaqui from his grandmother, his father's mother who lived in Guaymas down on the west coast of Mexico.

He learned English in school and his friend, who was an Arapaho from down around Riverton was teaching him his language too. "And, of course," Ramon told me, "don't forget Horse. I speak Horse too. But when I want those horses to know how much I love them, I sing it in Spanish. Like I do for you."

"So I'm as important to you as those horses?"

He laughed and hugged me. "You know it."

He had fun with English idioms too, those sayings that often make little sense to someone new to the language. I would wrack my brain to come up them since he enjoyed it so much.

"My dad got fired again," I said. "They gave him the boot."

"Only one boot?" Ramon asked. "Does he have just the one leg then?"

"He gets fired a lot, and he complained a lot, but he didn't have a leg to stand on."

"Oh, my God," Ramon said. "He lost both legs?"

"It's raining cats and dogs."

"Oh, my God," he said, "not another hurricane. I was down in Acapulco one time in a hurricane and it was literally raining cats and dogs. And trees and pieces of houses too."

"You can lead a horse to water, but you can't make him drink."

"You don't have to. If he's thirsty, he will drink. What does that mean?"

"I don't know. Maybe something about how stubborn people can be. That's a horse of a different color all right."

"Palomino? Roan?"

"Here's one for you. Wild horses couldn't drag me away from you."

"Or me away from you," he said, even though we both knew those horses he had to break always kept us apart.

Once when I was teasing him about his ideal woman, he said, "That's easy. A mermaid."

We were riding along the irrigation canal that day checking for places where debris had gathered to stop the flow of the water. He was riding one of the horses he had rough broke and I was riding a gentle old mare named Annie. We must have been about fifteen.

"Why a mermaid?"

"Practical reasons," he said.

"What practical reasons?"

"She could fish for her own food, would only need a pond to live in or even this irrigation ditch and when she dies, I can just flush her down."

I told him that sounded cold and mean.

"Would you rather I said the name of some real girl? And there's no good answer to a trick question like that. I learned that from my dad."

I learned new things from Ramon's dad too. He was always polite to me and he sometimes saddled my horse for me when I was going to go riding. Ramon told me that his father had the names of all seven of his children tattooed on his chest over his heart, even the one catch colt his extracurricular girlfriend had, his own private mermaid, the one that nearly drove Ramon's mother home to her mother. Of course, I never saw the names because Arturo was very formal. He would never take his shirt off around anyone, especially not his son's girlfriend. Ramon told me about the tattoos.

He said that of course his name was first, then his two younger brothers, and the extra girl's name which was Graciela was right in the middle. Her name was followed by the three youngest ones. All three of those names, Ramon said with a giggle were very long. The first one was Maria de los Milagros. His mother said that was the right name because it was indeed a miracle that she ever took his dad back after that unholy infidelity whose name was immortalized right over his left nipple. The next name was Emiliano Alejandro Cortez, followed by the last one, Annunciation Epifania.

"Mom wanted to get even with dad and make him feel some pain with those tattoos. My sister Epifania was the last one. Mom said she had an epiphany, that Mary herself, the Holy Mother of God, or maybe it was the Virgin of Guadalupe, told her to have no more kids. There was no more room on the old man's heart."

Sometime in our junior year of high school, everything in our relationship changed again. It became very intense and passionate. I began to spend more and more time with Ramon and his family. We would ride together every weekend. One day as Ramon was saddling our horses, he whispered to me, "Look. I stole it from my dad's dresser drawer." He held up a foil wrapped condom. "If the Pope knew about this," he said with a grin, "my parents would be assigned to hell. So I think they will say nothing even if they notice it gone."

We got on our horses and rode off together to the big hay field. There was an old shed at the edge of the field where the hay bales were stored for winter feeding. Ramon tied the horses up inside the shed so no one would know we were there. He untied the bundle on the back of his saddle. It contained one blanket and one white sheet. He took my hand and led me to the ladder to the hay loft where there was a pile of loose hay. He spread the blanket out on the hay and placed the sheet on top of the blanket. "That's one scratchy old blanket," he said.

We had been kissing and touching for a long time and both of us knew something had to happen. My body was trembling with anticipation and just a hint of fear.

When he touched me, especially that soft caress on my bare shoulder, I would become a mindless mass of protoplasm whose only purpose was to receive that touch. So this was inevitable. When it was over, Ramon held me tight and said, "Wow. That was short, but what else could we do? I think we would have died if we didn't do it. Next time it won't be that short. You know?"

I knew. I wanted to do it again and I knew I would keep on wanting to do it again and again. Ramon said it was like heroin, an addiction.

"We have lots of time," Ramon said. "Let's just stay here a while. The horses are okay. Everything's okay. Dad always says that if you find love, take it, that's what life is for. I usually don't agree with any damn thing my old man says, but he's right about that."

It only took me about fifty years to understand that everything that had gone between us before that day in the hay loft had been foreplay. No wonder it happened so fast.

And like Ramon said, it was never so fast again. Almost every time after making love, I would feel smooth all over, like God had ironed me or as though every cell in my body had been rearranged. I don't know any other way to describe that feeling and no one but Ramon could ever make me feel like that.

Ramon and I agreed that, no we didn't really invent sex, those billions of other people on the planet shot that idea down, but we did perfect it. And of course, we didn't invent love, but we sure lived it.

One day early in the fall of our senior year of high school, I saw Ramon smile and speak to another girl. He seemed so happy to see her. I felt a stab of envy that felt like it might kill me. I didn't know what to do, but the next time we were alone together, I made love to him as though we could be dead by noon tomorrow. That's when I knew without a doubt that I was in love, and it was as irrational and unpredictable as anyone ever said. And I could hold those two opposing thoughts in my head like a real mental patient. The textbook for the psychology class I was taking calls that phenomenon cognitive dissonance. The two thoughts were: One, we're in love and it will never end and Two, oh, God what if he loves someone else and it's over. I was not totally sane, but still it was wonderful.

Near the end of our senior year of high school, my dad told my mom he had done his share(three whole months on a job before he got fired)and it was her turn, completely overlooking the fact that it had been her turn the seventeen years before that, but she enrolled in summer school to renew her teaching license anyway. That left me with my dad.

I started looking for a job. I found one as a receptionist, research assistant and all-around flunky, coffee maker and errand girl for a law firm. The pay was good and I needed to gather up money for college expenses not covered by my scholarship.

I liked the job even though the two lawyers, a man and his wife, the Baileys, were always fighting with each other. I began to think it was very convenient that they were lawyers so they could litigate their own divorce which seemed highly likely to me, considering how they were always arguing and angry.

I learned some things there. First and most important, I learned I didn't ever want to be a lawyer or paralegal or anyone in any way associated with the practice of law. I did a lot of reading about law cases and law practices and I watched the Baileys work. It seemed to me that a lot of time was spent looking for, using and justifying the use of loopholes. It occurred to me that those loopholes were intentionally inserted into the legalese quite often. The Baileys could call their practice Loopholes, Inc. On the other hand, they were good to me and understood that I would leave for college in the fall and still they hired me.

It had also occurred to me that, at this rate, I could perhaps eliminate most occupations known to man in maybe fifty years and still not know what the hell I want to be when I grow up other than

Ramon's lover. I missed him. He would understand exactly what I was talking about and he would think it was funny, not pathetic.

Ramon drove the cattle up to the top of the mountain soon after school let out in May. He hugged and kissed me and asked his father if he would bring me up to stay some weekend.

Arturo looked at me, then at his son. "Yes, mijo, I can do that. I'm going up this weekend. Will you go?" he asked me.

I said I would. He picked me up at noon. The Baileys let me leave early and gave me a bonus in cash so I could help pay for the gas for Arturo's old pickup. On Saturday, Arturo took over Ramon's work duties, gave us the keys to his pickup, a twenty-dollar bill and told us to go have a good time.

Ramon drove to a lovely, secluded waterfall about half way down the mountain where we ate the lunch we brought and found a shady patch of grass where we could lie down. Neither one of us wanted to do anything else but hold each other. I told him I had missed him fiercely. "I don't know how I'm going to be able to go for a whole semester without seeing you," I whispered.

"We're going to start building our house in the fall after I bring the cattle off the mountain. Think about that. We'll soon have our own home. I'll do the bedroom first."

He whispered to me that he had no condom today. I whispered back that I didn't care. I had been having those longings or whatever it is that nature does to a woman. I wanted a baby. I had been telling myself, oh, hell no, not now, you're going to school, but I kissed him some more and whispered, "It's okay."

Even though I had nothing to compare it to, I knew this love Ramon and I shared was a rare and precious thing and that made me fear I would lose it. Ramon would hold me and say "Don't worry, you will never be rid of me. I will eventually become that gift horse you should never look in the mouth that you told me about. You'll be wishing I would take a trip, go out for a pack of cigarettes and never come back."

"You don't smoke."

"Okay, a quart of milk. I will never leave."

Still, I worried.

Arturo took me up on top of the mountain two more times that summer. One day in early August with less than a month before I had to show up for college, Arturo came into the lawyer's office. I was busy doing research on cases about water rights and usage in that part of Wyoming. I had learned that another very important facet of lawyering, along with loopholes, is the precedent. The Baileys were always looking for a precedent for whatever it was their client wanted. I found that very odd. Just because some judge somewhere declared something once in some case doesn't mean that it's right. I have much the same attitude about tradition; just because all of society has done something for years or centuries doesn't mean I should do it, or even that they should have done it.

Nevertheless, I was digging through a bunch of dry, old law books when Arturo came into the office. He took off his straw hat and stood quietly looking at me. I took one look at his kind face and knew that something was wrong. I got up and went around my desk and we went outside together where he told me that Ramon had been bucked off one of the horses he was breaking, hit his head on a rock and died instantly. They were bringing his body home tomorrow.

I couldn't think or speak. I heard someone wailing and sobbing and I realized it was me when Arturo put his arms around me and held me. I was numb with grief for days, all through the funeral and for days afterward. I wanted to kill that goddamn horse, that wild horse who had taken Ramon from me. I was angry and miserable and irrational and I had no idea what to do with any of it and I could not stop crying.

Arturo suggested that I stay with him and the family until it was time for me to take the bus to school. I told my dad I would be staying with Ramon's family and that Arturo would make sure I got to Laramie on time. We bought him a case of Budweiser and he was happy.

"Come. Let's go home. That will make us feel better."

He was right about that. The presence of Ramon's little sister, Epifania, was particularly comforting to me. She had idolized him and felt his loss as deeply as I did. We rode the horses together every afternoon we could. She liked to have me fix her hair for her and do her nails. I designed a dress for her and told her that I would make the pattern and sew the dress when I came home for Christmas holiday. It was only a couple of days before I had to go register for the fall semester in Laramie. I had been designing clothes for a long time and had taken a home economics class where I learned how to use a sewing machine.

All of Ramon's family and I were sitting outside in the cool, quiet evening watching the stars and the Milky Way. Juan Carlo, the brother just two years younger than Ramon was smoking a joint under the cottonwood tree. Juan Carlo had the same lovely golden sand colored skin that was Ramon's, but he wasn't happy and light hearted like Ramon. All the girls were crazy for him anyway, that dark brooding Heathcliff stuff that girls like, I think.

"Bring it over and share," Emiliano yelled.

"Not the little girls. Just me and her," he said to his father who was sitting by me. I realized I could understand most of, well, some of his Spanish, but Arturo asked Epifania to translate what he was going to say to me. She sat down beside me and listened to her father with an intent look on her lovely face. She looked so much like Ramon, it almost made me cry just to look at her.

After a bit, he stopped speaking and they both looked at me. Epifania spoke. "My father said you are family now. You must return here. You loved Ramon too and as his mother says, if we share this grief, we will lessen it." Epifania stopped and drew in her breath with a grin.

"He says he will demonstrate his deep love for you by adding your name to his heart."

I started to cry, and then both Epifania and I began to laugh. "My whole name?" I said. "It's not just Vangie. It's Evangeline Antoinette. That's a lot of pain."

"Then Mama will be pleased too," Arturo said in very good English.

"Yes, I like that," I said with the tears running down my cheeks. "And I'll be home for Christmas." I repeated it in Spanish.

MOM AND THE 38 SPECIAL

This whole damn embarrassing mess is Henry's fault. Yeah, Henry, my dumb little brother. He's never been diagnosed like some of the rest of us, but he has some screw really loose. Unpredictable is okay, but Henry always takes it to the absolute end.

He's the gun enthusiast in a family of mostly non-violent, anti-gun people. He owns a lot of them. Mom has always been anti-gun and anti-war, and Henry knows that as well as I do, so he has no excuse for talking her into owning a handgun.

We talked it over, but not until after she had already bought that 38. She and Dad had been divorced for forty some years and she was now living alone. Henry finally moved out several years back when he finally got through school and got his degree. In accounting. That startled everyone in the family. As far as we all knew, Henry wasn't interested in much of anything but drugs, booze and women, what he called the Holy Trinity or sometimes the Trifecta of Joy to which Mom would always add, Joy, my butt, more like the Trifecta of Jail. And he was never good with anything to do with math. So why accounting? Nobody knew for sure, but we all suspected that he made those decisions just like he made every other decision; while drunk or stoned, after consulting the I Ching. It was like a miracle that he finally graduated from college and it only took him nine years.

Joyce Keveren

After he moved out, Mom just kept living in her small house in an old neighborhood in the heart of Phoenix. The house was paid for and she had enough income to pay her expenses with a bit left over for a vacation trip to see her sister in L.A. once a year. She had her book club that met twice a month, her crochet group and her cable TV. Henry and I both thought she was happy.

Then there were a couple of murders in her neighborhood and Henry got paranoid. We were sitting on her patio one fine February day when Henry said, "Ma, you need a gun."

"What? I need a what?"

"A gun."

Mom laughed. "What in heaven's name for? Jake died. Didn't I tell you? I don't need a gun."

"Jake died?" I asked.

"Focus, Arnie," Henry said to me.

"When did Jake die?" I asked, ignoring Henry.

"About six years ago," Mom said. "I googled him. I kept saying I didn't care if he lived or died and I guess I meant it. It took me six years to find out and I wasn't even that curious."

Jake was an old boyfriend of Mom's, the one with the tattoo of a brain on his bald head who turned out to be a violent mean drunk, so she got rid of him. She had to move for a few months to do it, but she did it.

"Jake's dead. I don't need a gun."

"This is America. Land of the free and home of the gun," Henry said. "So Jake's dead? Wow."

"Yes, he's dead," Mom said. "And why are you calling him Jake now? Out of respect for the dead? You never had any respect before."

"That's not like you, Henry," I said, just to stir stuff up. "You always used to call him Dildo."

"Shut up, Arnie," Henry said with a snarl. "Jake's dead," he said. "Wow. Arnie and I had often talked of killing him, shooting him right through that medulla oblongata tattooed on his head. Now we don't have to."

Henry kept rambling on, talking statistics. "There are 393 million guns in America. And shootings every day." He took a crumpled up, dirty piece of paper out of his pocket and read from it. "U. S. citizens own forty-six percent of the 857 million firearms in the world. We have more guns than people. Why? you ask."

"I didn't ask," I said.

"Because we need 'em. There are shootings every day."

"No, we don't," Mom told him. "We wouldn't have shootings every day if we didn't have all those guns. I read statistics too. Seventy-eight percent of the country's guns are owned by three percent of the people so a small amount of people have a lot of guns, but most of us don't have any. How many do you have, Henry?"

"I've only got four, no wait, five now. I finally got that AK-47 I've been wanting."

"What the hell do you need an AK-47 for?" I asked.

Henry glared at me. "What do you need that goddamn boat you bought for?"

"I like that goddamn boat," I yelled.

"Well, I like my guns too. I go to the shooting range and I practice. It's a hobby and it just might come in handy too."

"Collecting stamps and bird watching are hobbies," I said. "Owning guns is a —well, not a hobby, it's an indication of some serious thinking problems. Paranoia."

"Nonetheless," Henry said pontifically, "I think Mom needs one."

He talked her into getting one too and took her to an indoor shooting range where she got very good with that 38 Special.

They found it at a pawn shop. It had some lovely mother-of-pearl inlay on the handle that Mom liked. Then he took her to an outdoor shooting range and she got so good with that gun that it made Henry jealous. Mom had always been good at sports that were one on one, like tennis and table tennis, water skiing and snow skiing, badminton, bowling and golf, anything that wasn't a team sport. He should have known she would beat him; she always did.

She got a new handbag with a little storage space that was just right for her new 38.

"What about your convictions about peace and no violence?" I challenged her one day when I was visiting.

"They're still there," she said. "Why?"

"Because of the gun," I nearly screamed. "You always hated guns."

"I know. I still do. Except for this one." She patted her purse. "I always liked that band too. 38 Special. And Henry's right. I do live alone. And maybe I do need protection."

"Or maybe everyone else around you needs protection now," I muttered. "Aren't you the one who always used to say there are too many guns around and then you would say 'Wouldn't it be a bitch if I was armed? How would you boys like that?'"

She laughed. "I did say that, but I think I can control those impulses now. And Jake's dead. And I learned how to use this nice little gun. It's different now."

"I sure hope so," I mumbled as I went out the door.

Then the November election rolled around and that old, ignorant, bloated, greedy, misogynistic, xenophobic, racist orange turd with the hideous combover was installed in the White House with the help of the Russian hackers just as if it was normal or business as usual. His skin was different shades of orange, so he must have been using a tanning bed or that tan in a bottle stuff or both. For a man who speaks like a white supremacist racist, isn't it odd that he tries to darken his white skin? It sort of belies the claim of white supremacy, don't you think?

And then, as everyone knows, everything went to hell in a shopping cart, one egregious offense after another. There was no time to breathe. The new president filled cabinet posts with people who promised to destroy every regulation designed to protect the environment and the people. Someone wrote a book called, Everything He Touches Dies. That was true. He took children from parents at the border and put them in cages. He paid off porn stars so they wouldn't mention his affairs with them and it turned out the porn stars had more integrity than he does.

He lied every time the camera was on him and I suspect every time it wasn't too. He pitted people against each other, he openly admired dictators and openly spoke of his desire to be dictator for life like his BFFS, some of the world's most brutal leaders. He appealed to the very worst in all of us; our greed, our fear, our hatred and our anger. He demonstrated over and over that he had no morals, no integrity, no conscience, no compassion and no shame. People all over the country were borderline insane from the shenanigans of this fucking idiot as some members of his Cabinet called him.

Mom was one of the people most adversely affected by the cruelties and stupidities of our commander in chief.

And it went on and on and got worse and worse. More women came out of the woodwork to accuse the man of improper sexual conduct through the years. Psychiatrists all over the country diagnosed him with Malignant Narcissistic Personality Disorder.

"Just like Jake," Mom said, "that consummate asshole. That orange boob in the White House is pissing all over the Constitution in his stupidity. He is destroying our democracy and I think he's doing it for Moscow." People all over the world agreed.

Henry and I and all of Mom's friends kept telling her to shut off the damn TV. She was watching way too much cable news and it was making her crazier and crazier by the day.

She didn't quit watching the cable news, but she did cut down on it and she also started going to the senior center in her downtown location.

"That's a great diversion," I told Henry. "Good for her. She's getting out and meeting people."

"Yeah," Henry said. "And you thought she was gonna die on the couch."

"She's ninety-one this year. It could happen anytime. And you have to admit she needs a break from the D.C. Shit Show. So it's all good."

Except it wasn't. Turns out the senior center had a TV room with soft chairs and recliners and a 60" TV screen where cable news played all day long, every day and into the night.

That's right. She was binge watching the Orange Menace's show day after day. She called him Our Pussy Grabber in Chief, rightly thinking that was one of his most offensive roles. The failed tycoon, the # One Biggest Loser of the 90's was another role he played, not one that a good actor would want to play, but a role nonetheless. And he played it well; his casino even failed. How in hell can a casino which basically has a license to steal, fail? Yet he pulled it off. After that, he became a reality TV star and is now starring in his greatest role yet, his own big show that I call the HA HA, I'm the President and You're Not Show. You can call it what you want.

I blame Reagan. He was our first show biz prez. And he, beloved, doddering old fool that he was, introduced that let-'em-eat-cake economic policy, the trickle-down theory. Problem is, the only thing trickling down on us poor people is piss, not money. He also introduced Alzheimer's and Mommy and all of that crap we endured while he was stumbling around eating jellybeans in the Oval Office.

And Mom was getting worse and worse. She was calling her representatives and senators in Washington with suggestions. You make the laws, you people, just make a new one that says his presidency is illegal, what's wrong with you? Are you all corrupt? The answer to that was pretty much yes, yes they are.

Margie, one of her friends from the senior center, told me in a stage whisper that could be heard all over the TV room if only they weren't all deaf, "Your Mom is bat shit crazy about all that political stuff. Of course, lots of people like your mom are crazy. I mean parents. I myself have no kids so I'm more sane. I'm startin' to think it's the kids. Yep, it's almost always the kids that make a parent crazy. Just take a look at those retarded spoiled kids of the Orange Menace if you don't think so." While saying this, she gave me a look that would have eaten holes in concrete. I repeated this statement to Henry, who, of course took it personally. It's like he doesn't know there's any other way to take anything but personally. I often wonder if Henry knows there are billions of other people here on this planet.

So he's nursing that massive injured ego and I'm wondering what the hell we can do to help mom who keeps insisting she needs no help from us. Then I realize for the 114th time at least, that there is little we can do to help her with this odd sort of pain this unqualified boob of a president is doing to everyone and everything he touches.

"Like Midas," Mom wailed, "but instead of gold, he turns everything he touches into shit!"

She got through the many episodes with him snuggling up to the flag with that idiotic grin on his ugly face like a fourteen-year old kid masturbating.

She got through the episodes where he snuggled up to brutal dictators he claimed he fell in love with.

Then he said he wanted to be president for life like the leader in China and she got through that. When he didn't get his way, like with the goddamn wall on the border, she saw him throw a fit like a five-year old. He threw twitter fits all the time, insulting anyone who dared criticize him, usually with untrue statements about whoever had hurt that blimp sized ego he totes around and covers with the stupidest combover in the history of mankind. She got through all of that. Margie said it was hard, she yelled and shook her fist at the TV, but calmed down with some mint tea.

It worried Mom no end that he was doing what all the world class dictators always did: try to kill off the free press. For without free speech, there IS no freedom, she reasoned quite correctly. She just kept getting by that too, Margie said, but she needed a lot of mint tea.

Mint tea? Why hadn't we thought of that? Nothing ever worked for me and Henry. I like to think it's Henry's fault, but it can't be all him. It's me too. Maybe Margie's right about her theory. Maybe, but mostly it's Mom. Her volatility is akin to that of Mt. Etna or St. Helens. We, I mean Mom and me, actually talked about this one time when I visited the senior center.

I told her, "You take a lot of crap from all these kids and grandkids and great grandkids and then, one day, like Vesuvius, you explode and scare us all."

"I know," she told me. "I know I do that. It's early training when women were supposed to do nothing but cook, clean, have babies, and keep their mouths shut because the men ran everything and we had no rights, like indentured servants. Now I'm trying to address every little thing and slight as it comes up, but I don't want to do that. It's exhausting. It's easier to just ignore it and then it tends to escalate because everyone around thinks I'm an easy mark and weak and pretty soon I'm dodging shit from every direction and my damn counselor died, so what to do? I have always counted on death to relieve me of all this, but that just ain't happening either," she sputtered.

Joyce Keveren

Then she pulled herself together, so to speak; she put her shoulders back and stood up, wobbled just a bit and headed for the bathroom. I figured she was okay.

I was wrong. She wasn't okay. Shortly after that, I learned that nearly everyone at the senior center was slowly being driven crazy by the news coverage of the President's mouth. They decided to shut the TV off and listen to music. That only lasted a few days until the Orange Menace started attacking Congresswomen of color, telling them to go back where they came from even though three of the four were from here and the other was a citizen. They turned the TV back on just in time to hear his rabid followers chanting Send Them Back.

I went back to the senior center after Margie called me to come see for myself how my mom was doing.

There were maybe fifteen old folks gathered around that gigantic TV, with maybe four or five who actually supported the star of the show, most of them men. Margie was right. They were at each other's throats and Mom was right in the middle of it all. One old guy kept yelling something about the Monroe Doctrine. "Don't need no new laws, these young fools don't get it. The Monroe Doctrine already covered all this flapdoodle."

I furtively googled the Monroe Doctrine. Turns out it was written by John Quincy Adams, not Monroe, go figure, and it pretty much says, 'All you Europeans get the hell out of our business here in the Western Hemisphere. NO MORE COLONIZATION! The old guy was sort of right. It should apply to the Russian internet trolls too, but it's a bit out of date. Then again, so are our leaders, the orange mess is at least a hundred fifty years out of date and so are the ancient senators who support him.

Of course, Mom was enraged, not by the old guy or Monroe for taking credit for Adam's work, but by every word that came out of the mouth of the Boob-in-Chief. "Now, he's attacking our inner cities, Baltimore this time. I live in an inner city and this is intolerable," she stated.

"Damn right," one of the other ladies said. "So he wants to be dictator for life. Somebody needs to tell the idiot that while we have impeachment and term limits to rid us of a bad president, the only way to get rid of a dictator for life is assassination."

"Not a bad idea," Margie said. The old men supporters of the president glared at her and one of them shook his cane in her direction. "Well, we've all been thinking it," Margie said defensively.

"He's not worth anyone spending one day in jail," Mom said.

They all agreed with that.

"Why not send in Bruce Willis or The Rock or maybe both of them? Stallone too," another old guy said with a chuckle.

"Maybe vote," screamed Margie. "Something possible."

"How about just shut the TV off again?" I suggested.

All of them slowly turned their heads to glare at me.

"We did that," Margie hissed. "And it didn't work. He's still there in the Oval Office, spreading hate." And just like the hatred in the Oval Office spreads like wildfire, the animosity in the senior center toward me was spreading too.

"Come on, Arnie," Mom said, steering me to the door, "Let's go home. See you all tomorrow," she called out to what had become a hostile mob.

Mom stayed away from the Senior Center for a few days, but she watched the show at home. She called me to tell me our leader's plan for dealing with the little problem with a Middle Eastern country he had been riling up with his rhetoric from Hell. "He said and I quote, 'I could fix this problem in fifteen minutes. But I don't want to kill millions of people.' Then he said it again about somewhere else, not Baltimore or San Francisco or L.A., all of which he labeled as real messes and it's no accident that all those cities are black, Hispanic or gay.

She forgot exactly what location he was threatening with the nuclear button, but she held on to how it made her feel. I tried to soothe her, but she just kept shouting, "That goddamn idiot is lying when he said he doesn't want to do that. They checked and they say he averages 16 lies a day. He can't not lie. And if I see one more little kid crying from being taken away from their parents, I don't know what I will do."

She got by that, but soon after that, there were two more mass shootings, both clearly related to the white supremacist rhetoric of the orange menace and he blamed the mentally ill. That enraged Mom because of all the mental illness in our family. But she finally got through that too.

Within a day or two, however, agents of ICE rounded up a lot of illegal aliens who were minding their own business working at some plant down south, leaving their children, most of whom were legal residents of the United States, alone, with no parents. There were photos and videotape of little children crying for their parents again along with the demented supporters of this cruel administration trying to justify this inhumanity.

It was a few hours after that when the call came from the Fourth Avenue Jail. It seems Mom needed bailed out. She was being held and the charges were willful destruction of property and resisting arrest along with unlawful discharge of a firearm.

"Resisting arrest?" I asked incredulously. "You're over ninety. How could you resist arrest?"

"Just bail me out and pick me up," she said. "The bail is $18,000. Just go to a bail bondsman."

"Eighteen thousand?" I screamed. "What the hell did you do?"

"Well, it seems that discharging a fire arm in the city of Phoenix is a felony. And, of course there is the cost of the damage too," she said mildly. "I have to go, another person needs the phone."

"What did you do?" I shrieked.

"Calm down, Arnie. I'll tell you when you get here. And I will pay you back for the bail money too." She hung up.

I found a bail bondsman and gave him my credit card and headed for the Fourth Avenue Jail and Mom.

I paid the fine at a little window in a small room with a few chairs lined up in orderly rows. Mom came out of a back room escorted by a young policeman. I stood up and went to her and she thanked the young man who blushed and hugged her back very gingerly. She is ninety-one and today she looked a little fragile. She was wearing a navy blue, long sleeved turtleneck sweater and a pair of heavy blue men's work pants with a short red wool jacket over all that blue and she had lost the rubber band thing she used to hold her long hair back so it was hanging loose all down her back and shoulders. It was pure white. She looked like the flag, red, white and blue, a walking ad for America. I guessed that may have helped her case because she was smiling. She had some papers in her hand.

In the car, I looked at her, a long appraising stare designed to intimidate her. I should have known better. She had always been unintimidatable.

"Thank you for coming out and picking me up. Thank you for paying the bond. I want to go home."

"If you run out and don't appear in court, I will kill you myself," I snarled. "What did you do?" I added with what I thought was very good, calm restraint.

"I don't think I like that tone, Arnie."

"All right. Please tell me what the hell you did, your highness, to need eighteen thousand dollars to bail you out," I said through gritted teeth.

She thumbed through the papers in her lap. "Well, it seems it's a class six felony to unlawfully discharge a firearm in the city of Phoenix," she said. "And of course, I am to make amends for all the damage."

"Damage to what?" I asked.

"Well mostly the TV that I shot up in the senior center and of course all the glass laying around and stuff like that."

"Of course," I muttered.

She read from the paper. "It says I am to buy the Saguaro Senior Center a new 60" TV, pay for all the cleanup and repair, and all or any injury, both physical or psychological to anyone in vicinity of said felony."

"Oh, shit, you didn't."

"And furthermore, I am never to ever go within fifty feet of the Senior Center ever again. And none of my children or grandchildren or great grandchildren either. Ever. In perpetuity. That's it. That's all."

"That's all?" I yelled. "Okay. Okay. Why did you do it? Why did you shoot that TV and what was on it when you did?" I briefly thought of Elvis shooting a TV in a Las Vegas hotel room and it had taken me about thirty years to find out who was on that TV. It was Robert Goulet singing. Not a bad idea altogether.

"You know why and you know who," Mom said with aplomb. That's the right word too. Look it up.

"The Pussy Grabber in Chief?"

"Yes, indeed. That's it. That's all."

So I drove toward home and I held my tongue in what I thought was superb self-control but Mom picked up on something.

"I'll pay you back for the bond. And they took my gun and I can't ever get another one."

"That's good," I growled. "I blame Henry."

"Well, it wasn't Henry's fault," she said belligerently. "I'm an adult and I bought the damn gun and I pulled the trigger right after I saw yet another child crying because a parent or maybe both parents had been deported. I was crying again and then there was our leader, shouting to a crowd, his mouth that looks like an asshole was wide open and he was screaming and sweating, and there was even snot dripping out of his nose, telling the reporters some more lies and—" She paused and rearranged the papers on her lap. "I don't know. I just stood up and I aimed at that mouth and pulled the trigger and that TV just exploded all over and all those old folks started yelling and clapping and hitting their canes on the floor and doing donuts in their wheelchairs. They finally started chanting Way to Go, Way to Go, Way to Go just like in one of the Pussy Grabber's awful rallies. I tell you, it was wonderful. Cathartic."

She was silent as I turned to look at her. "What?" she asked.

"What the hell do you think what?" I yelled. "I just picked you up at the P. D. And you're ninety."

"Ninety-one," she corrected. "I already thanked you for that." She got her checkbook out and wrote a check for the bail bond plus fifty extra and handed it to me. "I would do it again," she said defiantly.

"Except now you can't. They took your gun. Thank God."

"God had nothing to do with that. It was the city."

"Oh, shit," I groaned. "You actually enjoyed this—this bullshit." I glared in her direction.

"Yes, yes, I guess I did. Not so much the jail and paperwork and judges and all that, but the TV. I was real careful, told all of them to move way back. They did. Real quick. For a bunch of old folks."

"When?"

"What do you mean, when? When I was gonna do it, of course. The whole room enjoyed it, even the supporters of that fool. Oh, I get it. You think it was premeditated, don't you?"

I pulled up in her driveway and she gathered up her papers and her purse and got out of the car. She walked around to the driver's side and motioned for me to roll the window down. I did it like a dutiful son. She put her hands on her hips and looked at me through the open car window. "Of course it was premeditated. I have been premeditating about it for three long years." She flounced off. Flounced is the right word even though she's ninety and the edge is off a bit.

I put my head down between my hands on the steering wheel. I would have banged it over and over, but I didn't want to trigger the horn. I did not speak, just laid there thinking I need to tell Margie she's wrong. It's parents who drive their kids insane. The silence laid between us prickly as a field of goatheads, those savage little three-pronged stickers of the high desert. I finally looked up. "You got a key?" I asked.

"Of course," she said with a smile. "Can you drive me to court on the 12th?"

"Of course," I said as I rammed the gear shift into reverse. "Of course."

OLD LOVERS

I don't know why I started googling my old lovers. Maybe it was because I heard yet another one of my old classmates had died and I do mean old. All of us who are still alive are in our mid-eighties, that time of life when your contemporaries start leaving the planet one by one and various areas of your body start complaining and go on strike.

After the old classmate who was sort of my boyfriend way back when we were sixteen and naïve, died, I started thinking about those old lovers, starting with him. There was no sex, not with him, hardly any kissing even, but I could remember his face and his awful jokes. There's another annoying thing about old age. I can't remember where I put my glasses yesterday, or the name of that damn poisonous plant from Afghanistan that I hate, but I can remember some bitchy mean thing my ex-husband said fifty years ago.

Then I began to think of all the others who followed that first boyfriend, ones not so innocent or naïve. There weren't that many, really, because it started in the mid-fifties, that miserable time of the uptight I like Ikers when women wore girdles and garter belts and our skirts had to be an exact length and we were considered sluts if a bra strap should accidentally fall out. I like it better now when we can wear what we want and not worry about impropriety, this time now when women are finally trying to become equal to men, when we know we can do anything we are brave enough to try.

Joyce Keveren

Of course, the next old boyfriend I thought of was that one I thought I had to marry. I was pregnant. What else could I do? It was the fifties and my religious family would not hear of any other solution, even if I had told them, which I didn't.

We'll call him Jim to protect the guilty. The innocent need no protection. He was a short man with a big chest like a fat tootsie roll that always preceded him wherever he went due to his belligerent and erect posture. Somebody must have told him to stand up straight when he was a kid, or, more likely, he was trying to compensate for being only five seven. He had heavy dark eyebrows that looked like a pair of evil black caterpillars Satan had stored on his head. They made him look like he was glowering even when he wasn't. But he usually was. Glowering and blustering were two of the weapons in his bully arsenal.

I have no explanation about why I got stuck with him other than he exuded some kind of sticky stuff like some malevolent insect and I got stuck in it. That and the stupidity of the young. I was an idiot back then.

And yes, you're right. I learned to not like him much after a few years of being subjected to his erratic behavior that consisted of him quitting one job after another and dragging me and the kid all over the country. His drinking problem, along with his aggressive, bullying behavior made everyone steer clear.

After he alienated most of the people in our home town, including both our families, he moved us to a little town in New Mexico where he got a job as a ranch hand.

I made one good friend there who helped me become strong enough to divorce him. I got a job working in the cafeteria of the elementary school where my son was enrolled.

It didn't pay much, but enough for a small apartment for the two of us.

Of course, Jim didn't let go and move on, even though moving on was his regular MO. He stayed and stalked me and tried to move back in with me, but I had developed an immunity to that sticky stuff or maybe my hatred neutralized it. That's about when I started calling him by a different name. Oh, to hell with it. His name wasn't Jim, it was Kent Gardner. I don't need to protect him anymore. He's dead so it no longer matters to anyone, probably not even him. I started calling him Kunt Gardner. He was a heavy-duty professional womanizer, even though he was a misogynist so that name fit.

I loved that divorce even though I was scared about surviving on my own, mostly due to the fact that he had been telling me for years how worthless I am, how I couldn't possibly live without his help. I didn't care. I was free! Free! It was just like taking a lid off a pressure cooker. Stuff erupted everywhere. That's how I got Martine, another old lover. That was a disaster. Not only was he pretty much worthless as a breadwinner even for himself, he was in the running for winner of the World's Worst Lover Contest, but even so, I kind of liked him.

We somehow got away from each other although I had to move to San Diego to do it. And, in between Martine and my move to San Diego, there was Daryl. Daryl was good to me and a great lover, but we weren't in love. Not even close. That was fifty years ago and I've been in San Diego ever since.

So I googled Martine first and what came up startled me. It was an obituary. I checked the date of death again---eight years ago. He died eight years ago and I didn't have a clue? That's right. I guess I was telling the truth when I said I didn't care what he was doing or where he was. So I googled Daryl's name and what came up was a web site selling his sculptures and right below that was an obituary for him too. He too had died eight years ago. I read it again. It surely was eight years ago. Wasn't that what Martine's obit said too? I went back to that page and wrote down the date, March 17, then compared it to the date about Daryl's death. March 17. WTF? They died the same day? That's a pretty weird coincidence, but there it was.

I spent a couple of days thinking about it, tried to find a longer obituary with more information, but couldn't.

Then I thought of Rachel, Daryl's sister. Rachel and I were friends; we liked each other and spent some time together even after I left Daryl, although we had lost track of each other after I moved to San Diego. She would know what had happened.

Joyce Keveren

I couldn't find her number anywhere so I called the number on the web site that sold Daryl's sculptures and asked for her number.

"This is it," the voice on the other end said. "I'm Rachel and I run this web site."

"Rachel, it's me. Emma. How are you?" We chatted a while and I finally asked her what happened to Daryl. She told me it was awful. Martine died of a gunshot wound and Daryl was stabbed to death. They found them on the kitchen floor in Daryl's house.

"It looked like Martine stabbed Daryl and then Daryl staggered over to the kitchen drawer and got his gun and shot Martine who fell backward and Daryl fell on top of him and that's how they were found, laying together with their blood mingling and congealing in a big puddle on the floor."

"Oh, my God," I said. "I'm so sorry."

"Yeah, it was bad. And the worst part was that it was Marie, Martine's daughter who found them. You remember Marie don't you?"

" Oh, no, that's awful. Poor Marie." When I was with Martine, Marie had been a young girl. We had spent a lot of time together and we liked each other.

"Yeah, it was terrible. For the record and statistics, they called it a double murder. Now Daryl's stuff sells for a lot. Nothing like death to raise the price of art."

"That's good," I said. "Not the deaths, the art prices."

"He left his work to me. Did he give you any of his pieces?" Rachel asked.

"He did. I have two of them, one is a Madonna and child and one is the Virgin of Guadalupe or the Virgin Mary, both done in that pinkish alabaster he used to get from Wyoming."

"They're worth a lot now."

"I'm glad, but I'm sorry."

Rachel laughed. "It's been a long time, Emma."

"Oh, right." I felt a bit of guilt for not caring enough to even know for eight years and I also felt a stab of nostalgia, something I usually try to steer away from. "I'd sure like to see you."

There was silence on the other end. Then Rachel said, "I don't think that's such a good idea."

"Why not?"

"Because, remember Martine's family?"

"Yes. I do."

"That pack of crazy drunks is still around and now there's a lot more of them. They didn't much like Martine anyway, but they say it's your fault."

"What's my fault?" I asked.

"Well, the deaths."

I let that sink in. "My fault?" I yelped. "I haven't seen either one of those idiots for forty or fifty years."

"It's because you—ah—were with both of them—"

"That's ridiculous. Neither one of them gave one damn about me. If I remember right and I do, they hated each other before I ever had anything to do with them. It was an old, old thing even then. I clearly remember that Martine was jealous of Daryl's sculptures. Martine was a painter who worked in oils, but he never sold anything. He used to brag about being like Van Gogh, thinking he had never sold anything either until I reminded him that Van Gogh did sell three or four before he died. To his brother, but they sold. Remember he and Daryl roomed together at that art school they went to. They were friends from grade school. This mess had nothing to do with me."

"Yes," Rachel said, "and I know that too, but Martine's family doesn't."

"They should." I started to laugh.

"What's so funny?" Rachel asked.

"I chipped a tooth the other day. I'm eighty-five. I have wrinkles everywhere. It would take a five-gallon bucket of that wrinkle erase stuff to even start to make a dent in mine. Even my eyelids are wrinkled. I'm a snaggle toothed old hag with long white hair. Yes, Rachel, I'm a real femme fatale, a dangerous woman, what in hell is wrong with Martine's family? They didn't even like him. Nobody did."

"They're bored and drunk and they watch too many revenge movies."

"I think I'll come visit. Do you have a couch?"

"I do and I'll be glad to see you."

Joyce Keveren

I flew into Albuquerque and Rachel and her grandson picked me up.

When we came over the hill and I caught first sight of the town down there under the mesa, I was glad I had come. I had loved that little town. I asked Rachel's grandson to pull over so I could look at the town below us. It was nearly sundown. July lay on the village like a fever. The rows of haphazard adobe houses squatted closer to the earth they were made of, shrinking into themselves in the lazy heat. Little half-hearted wisps of dust were raised by an on again off again breeze off the river below.

Even the cottonwood trees looked lazy and heat tired, their leaves drooping.

"We can go now," I said. "I'm glad I came." I hugged Rachel before we got back in the car and she said she was glad I had come too.

"You can look at all Daryl's work. He left it to me in his will. Maybe he knew that it would be valuable someday. But there aren't many left. And we'll try to keep you away from Martine's family."

Rachel's grandson laughed. "Good luck with that. They're scattered like horse turds all over the valley. You can't avoid them."

"They'll never recognize me. I'll be okay. If they want revenge, all they need is patience. I'll be dead soon enough."

Rachel and I had a wonderful time. She drove me all over town to see the many changes. We drove to Santa Fe to a gallery that was selling some of Daryl's sculptures on consignment. One of them looked like me or the me I was fifty years ago. I would have bought it, but it was priced at fifteen thousand dollars. I thought about sending them my two Virgins to sell on consignment and took a card so I could call them. Rachel offered to try to sell them on her web site too.

Rachel cooked pots of posole with green chiles, enchiladas and burritos. We visited Taos and all its galleries. We watched TV in the evenings and the two weeks I had planned to stay were almost over.

On the night before I was to leave for Albuquerque to catch the plane home, we were sitting on the front porch of Rachel's house, enjoying the cooling air when all nine yards of Martine's relatives showed up. There were six guys out there, some of them were Martine's sons, and some nephews and most likely grandsons too, all of them drinking, some of them very drunk.

Rachel stood up and told them to leave when Marie, Martine's oldest daughter ran up in front of them all. She was an elderly matron of around sixty now, not the willowy young girl I had known, but she still looked tough. "Go home and sober up," she yelled at them. "All of you. Leave Emma alone. Now!"

I looked the men over. Sure enough, two or three of them looked a lot like Martine, who had been a good-looking man when he was young. They were all glaring at me, trying to intimidate me. It was working a bit.

"Go get the gun," Rachel whispered to her grandson.

"What gun?" he said loudly. "We don't have a gun."

"Hush," Rachel said. "That was a bit of comedic relief."

"It didn't work," her grandson said.

A couple of the least drunken ones heard the word gun. "Gun? Who's got a gun? I'll kick his ass." He took a step forward.

Marie was standing in front of them, her hands on her wide hips. They knew that meant business. "Shut up, Arnie. Go home. All of you."

"We want some answers," another one yelled. He looked straight at me. "What about it, Emma? What happened here? It's your fault our dad got murdered, isn't it? It's your fault this stain is on the good name of the family."

The good name of that family? What in hell can they be talking about? That ship had been in dry dock for sixty years. I shrugged and stood up and grinned so the snaggle tooth would show. It made me look like a wrinkled, ornery six-year old. "Yes, it's me, the love goddess of the Western World in the flesh. Men fight to the death over me. Helen of Troy reincarnated." I turned around like a model.

Rachel and her grandson laughed and Marie turned around to take a look at me. She smiled at me and then began to laugh too. "She's got a point," she said to her brothers and nephews.

"She wasn't always this old and fucked up," the meanest looking one said. "We want answers. And remember, we all know she slept with both of them." He was glaring right at me. He shoved Marie and walked up to the porch.

"Other people's sex lives are none of my business," I said with what I thought was haughty defiance.

All six men were looking at me now. Then they looked at each other. "But this is YOUR sex life we're talking about," the skinny one said, a perplexed look on his face.

"My sex life is none of my business either," I said while thinking what sex life? I could barely remember the one I had fifty years ago.

Some of the men looked puzzled. One of them started to laugh. The skinny one advanced another step or two closer to the porch.

Rachel took her phone out. "Back off, Jackson or I'll call the cops," she threatened.

"You want answers," Marie growled. "Then move back and I'll give you some answers."

"You don't know anything, Marie," one of them said.

"You forget. I was there. I know what happened." She walked up the four steps to the porch where we were sitting, then looked down at those six men.

"We just want to talk to her," the old one, who seemed to be the ringleader, said. "Now."

Marie looked down at them, for all the world like Evita Peron addressing the Argentinians. "You listen to me. This was all Dad's own fault. He started it, he's the star of this show."

"No way," one of the young ones said in a threatening tone. "Get out of our way."

"All right, goddamn it, you asked for it," Marie said, "but you're not gonna like it one bit. You forget. I WAS THERE. Now shut up and listen." They shut up and listened. "Martine was drunk like usual and I watched him stagger around the yard, muttering about 'those sons a bitches' and I saw him put that old hunting knife he likes and keeps sharpened into his boot so I followed him thinking he was headed for trouble again. He went right to Daryl's house and banged on the door. Daryl let him in. The door was open so I went up to see what was going on and Dad asked Daryl for some money. Daryl said something like, 'No, you're drunk, Martine. Go home. I've got no money for you today. You never pay me back.'

"Then Dad yelled, 'There are two kinds of people in this world, those who help their friends and those who don't.'

"Daryl laughed and shoved Dad. 'Martine,' he said, 'that's stupid and meaningless. And you're an idiot. Nothing personal. No offense, you understand, but anytime a sentence starts with the words, there are two kinds of people, it's just apt to turn stupid. Let me give you an example. There are two kinds of people in this world, those who fuck dogs and those who don't.'

"Then Dad howled and got that knife out of his boot and lunged at Daryl and stabbed him. Daryl grabbed his stomach and the blood was pouring out while I was running toward them, shrieking and crying. Daryl took a couple of wobbly steps over to the kitchen drawer and got the gun and shot Dad and Dad fell over backward and Daryl fell on him. I saw it. I heard it," Marie yelled. "Daryl's last words were, 'You dog fucking asshole, you've killed me!' So I figure it was true. So you bunch of fools who are so worried about tarnishing our good family name need to go find that goddamn bitch dog that caused all this. Along with Dad of course. You kill her instead of Emma. Leave Emma alone."

One of the younger men standing there was counting on his fingers. He looked up at Marie and said, "That dog's surely dead by now, Marie. That was," he stopped to think, "sixty or seventy years ago."

"I myself am," I thought a bit, "almost six hundred in dog years."

"Yeah," another one agreed. "That dog's dead."

"Then go home," Marie screamed. "It's over."

I didn't know whether to laugh or cry or vomit, so I laughed. Those six relatives of Martine's hung their heads and turned around and slunk off as Marie yelled at them.

Rachel started laughing and Marie looked at us and then she started laughing too.

I hugged her and said, "I'm so sorry. That was a terrible thing for you to witness."

"Yes, it was," she said. "But it's over now and I am so tired of hearing those brothers and cousins of mine bitch and whine about how you destroyed the integrity of our freaking family, Emma. It's been eight years. I had to do something."

"I can see that," Rachel said. "Come on in for a cup of coffee. You can visit with Emma. Was that all true?" she asked Marie.

"Every goddamn word," Marie said with a grin as she followed Rachel into the house.

SYLVIA'S WORDS

Most stories are made of words, but this one is about words too. My friend Sylvia told me this story, but not until she had downed three glasses of Chablis at that grungy cowboy bar in Scottsdale where she liked to hang out, mostly I think because of Jimmy, the handsome young Pueblo bartender who told her stories of reservation life in a mixture of his Pueblo language and English with a little bit of Spanish flavoring.

Sylvia told the story reluctantly, the words coming into being with pain and anger, pushed out from somewhere deep within her where she had been storing and keeping, hiding and nourishing them.

All of Sylvia's stories needed to be edited as her vocabulary was quite liberally laced with swear words, curses, pejoratives, invectives, scatological references, four letter words from at least three or four different languages and various other colorful obscenities.

She had told me a long time ago when we first met that she had cultivated the habit of speaking in obscene tongues. "It's a hangover from my younger days, the days of teen rebellion. All my family members were strict, upstanding Fundamentalist churchgoers and bad language was a real no-no to them, a transgression of the first degree, probably a remnant from those puerile idiots, the Victorians who couldn't even say leg for fear of getting horny, or more likely, fear of someone discovering their horniness even though they were multiplying like a bunch of minks which should have been a clue. But who the hell knows what that was all about?"

Joyce Keveren

"I think maybe it was also a class and control thing," I said. "The Victorians used speech itself as a clear indication of class, since the French Revolution and all those headless people, not to mention the American Revolution had sort of muddied up all the old class distinctions."

"You would think that with shared DNA, class distinctions wouldn't be a factor in my freaking case with my freaking family," Sylvia said as she ordered yet another glass of the Chablis from Jimmy. "When I was rebelling, I thought a bit about the options among the taboos of the super religious and I chose the bad words one as it seemed to me to be the least harmful, yet oddly enough, the one that got the biggest response."

"Good thinking," I agreed. "And way less harm to you too than some of the others like tattoos, or extramarital sex which can lead to all sorts of problems like chlamydia and babies. A hell or damn here and there sounds pretty innocuous to me compared to the really Big Sins."

"That's what I thought too. It wasn't nearly as hurtful or harmful as the pious, self-righteous condescending bloodlettings I had heard from them, even in church.

"When I was four, my mother spanked me for saying Judas Priest," she said. "Where but in church could I have heard it? That was before the band named itself Judas Priest.

"When I was around ten, I got my mouth washed out with soap for goddamning something. In retrospect, to be fair, it is worse to invoke a curse from a Divinity, real or imagined and who the hell can tell the difference, than to say fuck you which in real words is something almost everybody really does want. But have you ever tasted soap? She used that old brand Lava, that stuff Grandpa used to wash the grease off his hands.

"When I was about fifteen, I was grounded and slapped for calling my drunken uncle an asshole. What they were teaching me is that it was all right for him to be a misogynistic drunk who was mean to my aunt but it wasn't all right for me to call attention to it. Basically, they were teaching me to lie. The hypocrisy and injustice enraged me!"

Evidently it still did. And obviously she was still rebelling because she often sounded like Lenny Bruce at a court hearing.

"Lenny Bruce was one of my earliest heroes," she told me. "He was trying to wake people up to their stupidities and hypocrisy too and live more honestly."

She liked being compared to Lenny Bruce.

"They tried to kill him," I reminded her. "And they put him in jail."

Sylvia was thirty-six that summer, divorced with an eighteen-year old son who was away at college, doing his own rebelling, mostly irresponsible partying and flunking and getting Sylvia to pay for it.

Sylvia was small boned and delicate with large, luminous brown eyes and dark brown hair with a few strands of gray she always wore cropped short by her favorite stylist, Enrique whose salon was just a few doors down from the street from the boutique where we both worked.

The boutique sold recycled women's clothing, most of it designer labels, most of it barely used; worn for one gala event maybe, and some had the new tags still in place, as though it had never been worn at all.

Sylvia and I suspected that in some cases, selling their clothes was a means to extra cash, albeit a dumb one, for some society women, as in the rumors of Jackie O, whose monthly clothing budget was larger than the GNP of some small countries.

The store was called Share the Wealth and the two of us had first shot at the Ungaros, Aldophos, Yves San Laurents, Chanels, Vera Wangs, Nicole Millers, Versaces, Stella McCartneys, whoever was the current darling genius of haute couture.

Sylvia was always lucky, luckier than me.

She wore a size four and there were always many size fours. We suspected ladies who were dieting or dreaming of dieting bought them as an incentive to become model lean and never reached their goal. In any case, we were well dressed, fitted out by the most famous couturiers in the world who had access to the best fabrics known to man.

We regularly blessed those women who consigned those beautiful clothes we got to wear, not to mention the designers and world class tailors who made them.

Sylvia always looked especially good. She was beautiful anyway with clear creamy skin, delicate even features and she had impeccable taste.

Joyce Keveren

She was also the best salesperson ever to be employed at Share the Wealth. We all worked on salary plus commission, and she invariably made the most because she knew how to convince a customer that the long, bias cut solid color Valentino was a better choice for her robust figure than the short, ruffled little polka dot number by Givenchy which was really not suited to her 175 pound fat ass frame.

Sylvia had the right attitude, she liked her customers, she had the right eye for line and color and style and she had the right words. She could outfit women of whatever age, size or shape so they would look their best.

Her customers would spend and spend and return again and again and again because Sylvia had the right words. I don't mean she had a practiced line learned from one of those huckster rap Sales Techniques for Success video guys with the blow dried hair and mind; she didn't, with her it was all extemporaneous and spontaneous, but she had the right words and, of course, that wonderful sense of style, fabric and design and a real appreciation and love of good clothing.

If her words were occasionally supplemented by her repertoire of the obscene tongues, they still must have been the right words.

Share the Wealth lived up to its name. The owners who were pleased with our work, which translates to: we made money for them, and they rarely appeared at the store and never interfered.

That summer day she told the story, she was dressed in a subtle flower print by Ungaro made of the finest cotton knit material available, cut in a masterful manner that accentuated curves where there weren't any, making its wearer feel so good that she moved with an easy grace and confidence. At least, those were Sylvia's words about her favorite dress and it was certainly true of her.

We ordered more wine and she raised her glass. "To Emmanuel Ungaro," she said with a grin. "That guy must love women. He sure knows how to make them look good."

"How was your vacation?" I asked. She had just returned from a week spent with her mother and sister in the little Bible Belt town where she had been raised and then rejected. "Just before they sacrificed me," she always added.

"To my mom," she said, raising her glass again. "And my sister Audrey."

I knew Sylvia had spent fifteen years in an unhappy marriage to a man who was possessive, jealous and mean, a man who never passed up an opportunity to denigrate and belittle her, a man her Fundamentalist family required her to stay with until death did them part, it's in the Bible, I'll show you, or the fires of hell for eternity will be your reward.

Talk about bad, scary words. And yet, Sylvia had made her escape; she divorced him, with no help or support and much opposition from her family, none of whom had ever been divorced.

In the three years I worked with her, she became the best salesperson there and she learned more about buying and selling and high fashion than anyone else who had ever been employed there. She was smart and fun loving, warm and hard working.

Her life, she said, had finally become good. She was happy and productive and independent. She was enrolled in night school studying fashion design, she loved to go dancing and had a lot of dance partners at the studio where she had taken lessons.

The healing was slowly but surely happening.

Yet here she was, reduced to her longshoreman's mode, spilling angry tears and curses into a glass of cheap bar Chablis after a short visit home.

That beautiful bartender, Jimmy, noticed of course. He kept going by our table to touch her hand, saying, "It's all right."

"In Jimmy's language," Sylvia told me, "there's just one word for the sex act and one for each of the other functions of the body, which we'd all be dead if we didn't do! One word, no shadings, no degrees, no value judgments, no class distinctions, just matter-of-fact, straightforward words. They are what they are. Like Popeye. I yam what I yam. It is what it is. No bullshit, no sugar coating."

"But I like the variety and expressiveness of English too," I said.

"Of course," she sputtered. "Or of any language. That's not what I'm mad about."

"Silly pretentious euphemisms?" I asked.

"Not that so much either. They're just silly."

"What then?"

"I don't know," she said. "Words, like Jimmy says are only symbols for something else, designed for communication, and when they become more than that, they become divorced from the reality of the thing they represent."

"Like people who live in penthouses and high rises are divorced from the land and they get weird," Jimmy volunteered. "Ain't no high rises where I come from except the mesas themselves."

"Language is always changing and evolving unless it's dead. And it's arbitrary! People make it up! Every freaking word ever uttered was made up!" Sylvia said.

"Of course," I agreed. "And the worst possible use of language is as a weapon. So what are you mad about?"

"Okay. Here's an example. Audrey's got three kids. One of them is a little kid still in Pampers. She and my mom sit around and discuss his diarrhea and his bowel movements, the color and consistency of his stools with nary a thought for those of us eating lunch, yet if I say shit, they cringe. Or even the word crap will get a reaction like I'm a mental leper. It makes me crazy! There's no difference. It's the same stuff! And my sister talks about trying to make another baby, what days she's fertile and so on and on. Like I really want to picture that in my head. Yet if I accidentally say one little widely used four letter word that is used as a noun, verb, adverb and adjective, you name it, that all-purpose word we've all heard of, have done or will do—if I say it—the same thing they're talking about, I'm a pariah, a fallen woman, not quite as good as they are, especially since my divorce. And I even think that a society that uses that word, which is the very act that perpetuates the species, for a curse is messed up and confused and pretty damn sick!"

"So you agree with your family then?"

"No!" she said. I don't. You don't understand. They use my language, my old habit of using four letter words, to criticize and ostracize me. That's what pisses me off! They do and have done what those words stand for but can't bear to hear the word. It's ludicrous!"

"Perhaps their standards are just different from yours," I suggested. I moved my chair just a hair's width away as I said it. Just in case.

"I guess so," she agreed mildly, surprising me. Then she added, "Who the hell's side are you on anyway? I wouldn't think of hurting my child like that over a damn silly thing like a couple of words!"

"Of course you wouldn't." I knew that much about her. "I was just playing Devil's Advocate."

"All right then," she said to me as she girded her loins to tell me the rest of the story.

And just how the hell does one gird a loin since we're discussing words?

"It's not a nice story, but here goes. My sister's husband, we'll call him Butthead for the purposes of this story, is, in keeping with family tradition, like my dad and husband before him, a manipulative, controlling, abusive bully who should be arrested for child and spousal abuse," Sylvia said.

I could barely hear her she spoke so softly.

"Butthead wandered home late at night when Mom and I were visiting. He was drunk and meaner than usual. He woke everybody up, me and Mom too and he lined Audrey and the kids up in the living room like he was Patton surveying the troops and he screamed and yelled at them.

"He said things like, 'I'm the boss of this house' along with all the bad words I had ever heard and some I don't even use. He's horrible, maybe even unbalanced, maybe a psychopath and the little kids were terrified. I was terrified. The bastard finally passed out, but I still couldn't get any sleep and the kids told me he does it a lot and he even hits them. Mom was moaning and crying over the bad words of course. That's what she noticed." Sylvia sucked in her breath and plunged on.

"Next day, my mom and sister act like everything's just fine and make plans for me to spend another night there. 'We'll go eat lunch at the Italian Garden and get things for dinner and go back to Audrey's,' Mom said. And I said, without even thinking, just feeling, 'I'm not going to stay there. Fuck that!' And my mom looks at me all aghast like I'd done something horrible, something unforgiveable like pulling legs off babies or killing the preacher. Then she says in a voice as cold and hard as hailstones, 'You're as bad as he is.'

Joyce Keveren

"I was so shocked to hear those harsh words comparing me to a child and woman abuser, I just shut up and went to get a motel room and a good night's sleep, feeling like I had just had a thousand cc. injection of guilt administered." She took a drink of her wine.

" 'Butthead was just upset and threatened by your visit,' Audrey told me the next day. So not only was I as bad as Butthead who beat his wife and kids, I had driven him to it. It was my fault. I got through the next three days of family visits and even went to church with them where I heard a sermon that quite effectively bashed everybody but their little flock, especially me since I fit into so many of their thou shalt not categories. Then the preacher comes home with us and corners me and Audrey in the yard and tells me I shouldn't have eaten the cardboard wafer and drunk the itty bitty cup of grape juice as I was not in a state of Grace, having been divorced. I was being told I was unfit to participate in a ceremony with cannibalistic overtones! And he tells me if I want to go to heaven, I better clean up my act and go back to my abusive husband and all the time he's spewing those acid-loaded words, he trying to feel Audrey up! On the sly! By now I'm so crazy from it all, I just mumbled something that sounded like gibberish even to me and escape to go pack my suitcase and come home feeling like I've been put through a paper shredder. I'm still all raw and ragged. And maybe the worst part is they say they're trying to help me!"

"Oh my God," I say. "Holy crap!" I tell her. "I'm so sorry, honey. But you're okay. You really are."

"I love you," Jimmy said with a grin. "You can talk any way you want to as long as your heart is good. It's the feelings that count, not the words."

To Jimmy's surprise, Sylvia burst into tears.

"You're right, Jimmy," she said when she had finished blowing her nose into a couple of cocktail napkins when the storm of tears was over. "It wasn't the words, was it? It was the feelings behind them that hurt. They have given me nothing but bad, hurtful feelings, no acceptance and no love.

Especially since my divorce. That's what hurts the most."

She was lost in thought for a while, her forehead creased and her eyes unfocused. Then she looked up at Jimmy and her face cleared like the airport waiting room when somebody yells, "BOMB."

"It was never the words, was it?" she asked in a voice filled with a mixture of sadness and delight. "It was just a lame excuse not to like me!"

"And that makes you feel better?" I asked in a tentative voice while trying to remember where the hell I had put the Dial-a-Shrink number.

"Sure. It does," she said with the sort of enthusiasm she usually saves for a size four Versace. "I can quit using those freaking words now."

I was frantically digging through the contents of my purse. Where the hell is that number? I know I had it written down.

"But you don't have to quit using those words," Jimmy was saying. "We don't care. We love you just the way you are."

"Thank you, Jimmy," Sylvia said with a calm dignity. She laid some bills on the table and stood up. "I have to go," she said abruptly.

"Why?" Jimmy and I asked almost in unison.

Sylvia smiled. "I'm all right," she assured us. "But I have to go home and call my kid so he knows that even though I know he's an irresponsible, selfish little screw-up, I love him anyway."

I gave up the search for the Dial-a-Shrink number and snapped my purse shut. It doesn't look like she needs any help. Sylvia is all right.

NOT LIKE HER MOTHER

Nicki was six the first time she vowed never to be like her mother.

That was the summer her mother Karen left her father, packing the three little children up and driving through the night to a shelter in Denver where they lived for a month while Karen filed for divorce, custody and child support.

Nicki spent her eleventh birthday in a motel in Albuquerque with her mother, her brother and her sister Charlene. She renewed that vow in that motel under a flashing neon sign as a cold, harsh wind blew out of the southwest.

The motel was two stories high done in mock Pueblo style constructed of cement blocks plastered over to look like adobe. It was painted a deep sienna brown with doors and window trim of an electric turquoise blue. The flashing neon sign outside said, "The Kiva."

Their room had two beds and a TV chained to a dresser. There was a swimming pool out back but it wasn't heated and it was still far too chilly to swim. It was April 6, Nicki's birthday. There was no cake, no candles and no presents for that birthday.

Nicki's mother Karen had risen at seven A. M. that morning, poured three bowls of cold cereal for the children, loaded them up in the car as usual, but instead of going to their school, she headed south out of the Denver suburb where they had been living with Karen's second husband Chuck. She headed for Albuquerque.

Karen had made no plans, had nowhere specific to go; she had simply got up and left. She left no note and no explanation for Chuck. She took some personal things like the old photo album from her Connecticut childhood, a couple of old dishes with hand painted roses that had belonged to her great grandmother, clothes for the four of them and a few toys and personal possessions for each child.

Charlene cried when she couldn't take her new red wagon, but it wouldn't fit in the trunk of the car even without the necessities.

"I'll get you another one," Karen promised. "Just as soon as the divorce settlement is over."

Nicki had heard those words before. Divorce settlement. She remembered them from five years earlier when they had left her father. Karen had woven them into a soothing lullaby to comfort Charlene in that shelter.

Karen had consoled Nicki at six by saying her father would come see them, she was divorcing him, she would no longer be his wife, but the children would always be his children and he would always be their father.

That was perfectly true of course, but her father moved to Alaska and they had only seen him once in all those years when he had come to visit with a new wife and son and the old children had become awkward strangers.

Nicki blamed her mother for that. She blamed her mother for inflicting that horrible Chuck on them, she blamed her for everything and the older she got, the more specific the charges became. No, by God, she would not be like her mother.

But she was glad to be out of the clutches of Chuck. He was a successful rancher who had looked like a good catch to Karen. He was handsome, lean and well off. He wore colorful, tight fitting western cut shirts with pearl snap buttons, sharply creased Levis, pointy toed boots and a wide hand tooled leather belt with his name on it and a big silver buckle.

Nicki hated him.

He had no children, which had been a positive attribute to Karen. There was no competition for her children to worry about she said.

Competition for what? Nicki wondered for Chuck was distant at first, then cold, then cruel. Not only did he not have children, he didn't want them. In time he became abusive, so once again Karen packed up and left.

She got a lawyer lined up who would assure her a settlement large enough to get them established somewhere else.

In that dingy motel room on her eleventh birthday, Nicki had the sudden realization that Karen had left her father for the same reason. He had been abusive too even though the children had been his own.

That revelation did not alleviate her anger toward Karen or effect a change in her thoughts. Karen, after all, had chosen those men. Nicki renewed her vow never to be like her mother there in the wind by the motel pool with last winter's fallen leaves floating on the chilly water under the flashing light of the neon Kiva sign.

Gradually Nicki began to see a pattern in her mother's behavior. After each divorce settlement, she would establish herself in yet another town or city where she would join clubs and organizations where she could meet yet another man to marry. After Chuck, there was Larry and after Larry there was Phil.

Karen made a career of marriage like some people make a career of the military and she became very good at it.

"My mother is a professional marrier," Nicki said to herself.

Karen learned never to allow her heart to overrule her head, not after that first one who was the father of her children. She had to be practical. She had to support those children. It didn't seem to occur to her that placing them in unpleasant situations, if not actual danger from abusive men who would then be sued by aggressive divorce attorneys was not a supportive gesture.

It made Nicki crazy even to think about it. She vowed silently and fervently that she would never be like her mother.

Then prenuptial agreements came into fashion and Karen was forced to end her career prematurely. Fortunately, the settlement from Phil, a wealthy contractor, was substantial enough to keep them all going for a long time. And Karen reasoned secretly to herself, perhaps real love with a good man was not impossible.

Joyce Keveren

Phil's generous settlement paid for Nicki's tuition at the University of New Mexico. It paid for her brother's braces and Charlene's high school needs. It paid for a small house in an old Albuquerque neighborhood down near the Rio Grande. There were two old cottonwood trees in the large backyard and yellow blooming forsythia bushes in the small front yard with its crumbling adobe wall.

Nicki stayed at home the first two years she attended UNM to save money. In her third year, she moved into a small apartment near campus which she paid for with her job in the work studies program. She could barely pay rent and buy food, but she was determined to become independent, determined that she, unlike her mother, would not live off abusive men. Ever.

She would find a career in which she could help people who couldn't help themselves, people like herself and her brother and sister, people at the mercy of others who were taking advantage of them.

She chose a career in physical therapy. She was not a big girl, only 5'6", but she was strong and capable. She could work for a school or a private athletic club, at a hospital or a clinic. She could establish her own service, set up an office or travel to the people who needed her services.

Eventually she chose to set up her own practice and went to the homes of her clients.

That's how she met Kenny. Kenny lived in a big home up on the side of Sandia Mountain above the city. The home had been built to his specifications to accommodate his wheel chair. It was paid for by a huge settlement he won in the court case with the insurance company that insured the driver of the car who hit his motorcycle leaving him a paraplegic from spinal cord injuries.

Nicki's job was to exercise the limbs so they would atrophy as little as possible. Soon she was exercising other appendages as well and then they were married.

The marriage enabled her to discontinue her work to devote all her time to the 6000 square foot mansion on the side of the mountain and to Kenny who was really not too demanding.

"He's gentle and sweet," she told her mother, as the unspoken words, not like your men, hovered in the air between them.

"Of course he is," Karen said. "He can't move."

Nicki soon hired other physical therapists to attend to Kenny's needs, took the Mercedes on long trips to Los Angeles, San Diego, San Francisco, anywhere she wanted to go.

She had unlimited freedom. She had credit cards, cash, clothes, jewelry, anything she wanted and Kenny always had good care. There were around the clock nurses and, of course, his therapist. Kenny was always glad to see her when she came home from one of her trips. She brought him shells from the beach and promised him a trip to the ocean. Kenny was gratified and happy, always glad to see her and never abusive. No, she was not like her mother.

They were packed and ready for the trip to the ocean when the automatic hydraulic lift that raised and lowered Kenny's chair into the back of the big van malfunctioned. It crushed the chair, it crushed the van and it crushed Kenny.

Nicki called 911 but it was too late. His wasted body was lifeless. She was screaming and crying when the paramedics arrived.

"It got stuck!" she wailed. "I couldn't stop it!" she screamed. "It malfunctioned!" She had to be sedated at the hospital.

Her mother came to the funeral as she had come to the elaborate wedding. She pleaded with Nicki to come home for a rest and a visit. Karen was between husbands and perhaps lonely. But Nicki wouldn't go. She preferred the big house with its Italian tile floors and huge windows overlooking the city.

"I need to mourn alone," she said. "I'm not like you, Mom. I don't need to surround myself with a bunch of people all the time, a bunch of men. I need to heal myself alone."

It was a rapid process, the healing. She was a grieving widow for only a short time. After all, Kenny would have wanted her to continue on and be happy. He had liked that about her. He had left his entire estate to her, the house, the Mercedes, the stocks and bonds his financial advisor had helped him to purchase when the settlement from the car accident was first granted. Kenny had been a wealthy man and now Nicki was a wealthy widow.

No, she was not like her mother. If ever she had children, she vowed they would never be subjected to anger and violence. They would never have to sleep in a crumbling motel after abandoning all their possessions while she was on the run from an abusive husband or boyfriend she had thought she needed. She could damn well take care of herself. She didn't need a man.

Except she became a bit bored. She would not go to Vegas for a hurried weekend of gambling, booze and men like her mother used to do. Never. She searched the want ads. Maybe she should go back to work, be of some use to the world.

That's how she met Philip. Philip had been injured in a ski accident at Vail seven winters earlier. His spinal cord injuries, he assured her, would keep him from ever walking again. He had limited use of his arms however. He was a paraplegic with a business he ran from his home. He had long since left behind any anger or bitterness about the accident or the wheel chair. He was only a few years older than Nicki who was hired as his physical therapist. He was handsome, with distinguished wings of gray at his temples and intense blue eyes full of intelligence, humor and kindness.

Soon she was giving him many different kinds of expert therapy.

When he asked her to marry him, she sold Kenny's house on the mountain, converted the stocks and bonds into cash and moved into Philip's 4000 square foot home fully equipped with internet services, cable and wheelchair mobility. His insurance company had also been generous.

Nicki was happy and secure. She was not like her mother marrying one abusive man after another just to survive.

One day she discovered Philip snorting cocaine off his adjustable food tray, his long, thin slightly twisted arms and hands awkward with the tiny straw.

He offered to share a line with her a couple times. "It eases the pain," he explained.

Soon it was also easing her pain. What pain? she would ask herself as she went shopping at the most exclusive shops in the city with her own credit card with its $25,000 limit. She could buy whatever she wanted with her own money anytime she wanted.

The problem was this: She didn't know what she wanted. She only knew what she didn't want. She didn't want to be like her mother.

"I'm restless, Mom," she said on the phone to Karen.

"Take a vacation," Karen advised. "Take a plane to Las Vegas for a week."

"I just got back from Cancun."

"Go shopping."

"I'm tired of shopping. I don't know what I want."

Karen cleared her throat and plunged ahead, knowing Nicki wasn't usually susceptible to advice from Mom.

"I'm not like you, Mom," Nicki interrupted defensively, her voice harsh through the phone lines.

"Maybe you need a man, Nicki."

"I have a husband."

"I mean a whole man, one who isn't a quadriplegic."

"Philip isn't a quadriplegic. What a cruel selfish thing to say. That's just like you."

"Paraplegic then. I mean a man who is a whole man."

"Like your men, Mom?" Nicki asked, acid dripping off the syllables, "with legs to kick you and hands to throttle you? No thanks."

Karen gave up, but Nicki thought about what she had said. Then a few months later, she discovered Ron, a physical therapist she met at a job conference and they started meeting in the best hotels in the city where they drank the best champagne and occasionally snorted the best cocaine.

Nicki paid for all of it from the sale of her house. Even though her account was slowly dwindling, she could still afford it. She was not like her mother, going from one pathetic, abusive man to the next so they could support her. Nicki bought Ron a car, a lovely little convertible they cruised around the city.

She had fallen in love for the first time in her life; there was nothing she wouldn't do for Ron or buy for Ron. The sex was heavenly, transporting her to another world. Maybe her mother had been right about one thing, her needing a whole man, one who could dance and run. Yet she doubted Karen had ever been so deeply in love. That was hers, Nicki's, only hers.

She became obsessed with Ron, sneaking him into the house she shared with Philip, hiding him in her walk-in closet when Philip visited her room, passing him off as the pool boy when Philip found them drinking margaritas together by the pool, she in her $300 designer bikini, Ron in his tiny white briefs, his long bronze body glistening in the sun.

When Nicki's money from the sale of her house was almost gone, she started using the credit card more often and paying on it less.

When the credit card company shut her off, she applied for five more. When those were maxed out, she asked Philip for her own bank account.

"My business has fallen off, Nicki. I can barely make the payments and keep the household running right now. Maybe you'll have to curtail your spending for a while."

"And maybe you'll have to stop snorting so much cocaine," she said angrily. That's where all the money is going, she decided. Up his nose while she could barely keep Ron around anymore.

The thought of doing without Ron's company, Ron's body, Ron's caresses, Ron's mouth, Ron's love was more than she could bear. She had to keep him. She was not like her mother, practically asexual, willing to live with any lame, limp scrap of a man to support herself. No, she would think of something.

There was no more money for the five-star hotels for her and Ron to make love in, so she started taking more chances by bringing him to her bedroom, locking the door and activating the intercom system Philip had installed in case he needed help. That way she would have time to get Ron out of the house through the patio door off her room before Philip could find him. That would work, she reasoned. She was not like her mom; she was smart. And how could it hurt Philip who was lucky to have a wife at all, especially one as devoted and kind as she was. She was always patient with him and still gave him all kinds of therapy, especially the kind he most craved that his daily therapist didn't do. She was not like her mother; she would not divorce him for Ron.

Early one morning when Ron had spent the night in Nicki's room and they were asleep amidst the tangled bedcovers, Philip's wheelchair rolled through the wide door they had, in their heavy passion, forgotten to lock.

There was no time to hustle Ron out the patio door, no time for talk about the pool boy.

Nicki got out of bed, her naked body still smooth and warm from sleep and lovemaking.

She grabbed a robe and wheeled Philip out the door while motioning for Ron to escape.

Though she tried, smiling her sweetest smile, using her softest words, Philip would not be placated.

"I'm going to call my lawyer and file for divorce," he said. There were tears in his brilliant blue eyes.

"I'll get a lawyer too," she said. "We can work out a settlement." She was startled, never having thought she would hear herself repeating the words of her mother.

"There will be no settlement!" Philip yelled. "You'll get nothing more from me!"

He wheeled angrily away from her. "I'm even changing my will!"

She spent the next several days catering to Philip's needs, not letting him out of her sight, soothing him, cajoling him, promising never to see Ron again. She drove him to his favorite restaurants, wore the dresses he had bought for her when they were first married, dismissed his current physical therapist and took over the routines herself.

True to her word, she didn't see Ron for the month it took her to convince Philip of her renewed devotion.

She did call Ron on her cell phone anytime she was away from Philip.

Ron was becoming more and more insistent that she see him. "Don't tell me you can't get away from him. He's in a goddamn wheelchair! I need to see you," he said, his voice full of anger. "I'll come there."

"No. No. You can't," she told him. "I'll come see you. I'll go shopping and come see you."

It became harder and harder to put Ron off. She had checked, very discretely of course, with Philip's lawyers to see if he had made any appointments with them. He had not, the secretary said. She went through the papers in his wall safe when Philip was out and there had been no changes to his will. Unless he had made another one.

Joyce Keveren

She met Ron at his small apartment one afternoon after telling Philip she had to shop for groceries and drop some dry cleaning off, run a few errands that would take only two or three hours.

She surveyed the cluttered mess of Ron's apartment, the pile of dirty dishes in the sink, the empty beer cans in the tiny living room, his dirty laundry scattered all around the bedroom and threw herself into his arms.

"We can't go on like this," she said between feverish kisses. "We need each other."

"Let's go out for dinner at that steak house," Ron said later. "I'll get dressed."

"I can't. You know I can't. Not now. Give me time. We'll be together soon." She was not like her mother, too eager for love, too eager to wait and plan.

She stopped at a travel agency on her way home and gathered up some brochures on Yosemite Park and stuffed them into her tote bag. Philip had always wanted to take a trip to Yosemite.

That night after a dinner of all his favorite foods, she cleared the glass and brass dining table of the dishes and food and laid the brochures before him.

"Let's go to Yosemite," she said as she caressed the face she had once again been shaving every morning.

He glanced through the brochures, his twisted fingers awkward with the slick, brightly colored folders.

"It would be too hard," he said with a smile at her. "We would have to take someone to help lift me in and out of the van, so it wouldn't be a holiday just for the two of us."

"I already thought of that," she said. "I thought of everything." She kissed the top of his head as she stood behind him. "I had the gardener take the van to a shop where they install wheelchair lifts. With a hydraulic lift, we can do it alone."

He turned his chair to face her. She was smiling as she reached down to embrace him. "That's a wonderful idea. You did think of everything."

"Yes," she whispered. "It will solve all the problems."

THE LAST ROOMMATE

From the time she left home at the age of eighteen to go to college, Melanie had roommates. She never stayed in a dorm where there would be a lot of roommates, none of whom she was free to choose herself. That didn't appeal to her at all. She was afraid that living in a dorm in the midst of so many strangers would only exacerbate her occasional bouts of paranoia or anxiety, yet she didn't want to be alone for the same reason.

She was between a rock and a hard place and the obvious solution was just what she didn't want: another roommate.

Melanie's Daddy, who was a successful dentist, agreed. He had been paying for a series of apartments for Melanie; always two-bedroom so Melanie and her roommate would have their own bedroom and some privacy. The roommates or their Daddies were required to pay half the expenses. That had not always happened in the past; frequently, in fact, Daddy was stuck with a big bill that required a couple of root canals to cover.

Predictably, Daddy got tired of it and quite vociferously requested that Melanie who was now in a graduate studies program either restrict her living quarters to a studio or one-bedroom apartment or pay for her own living quarters. He would no longer pay for her deadbeat roommates, male, female or whatever. No more.

The last one had been male. All the others were female. Both Daddy and Melanie had lost track of how many there had been in the last six years. Some of them had been reduced in Melanie's and Daddy's minds to labels. There was The Snorer, a med student who popped pills, slept at odd hours and snored like a 747 coming in for a landing.

There was The Militant Vegetarian who ate little except soybeans, yogurt and alfalfa sprouts and required that all those around her, especially those she lived with, do the same.

Daddy swore that she became more bovine-like every time he saw her. Melanie just lost weight.

There was The Cellist who practiced constantly which was virtuous, yet never improved which was uncanny.

There was The Nazi who was a germ-fearing freak who flew into rages over dust bunnies and stray food scraps.

There was The Nympho whose bedroom door was revolving.

There was The Witch who was a card-carrying member of Wiccan who held coven meetings in her room from time to time.

There was The Actress who was enrolled in a performing arts program who turned her whole life into a role.

There was The Junkie who only OD'd once in the six months they lived together and there was The Saint who was an expert in Judgmentalism, having learned it at a Revivalist Church and, of course, there was The Lover who always had at least one woman in addition to Melanie herself. So, Melanie as well as Daddy was a little disenchanted with the roommates herself.

"Melanie," Daddy said with just a hint of exasperation in his voice, for she was his first born, his darling, his favorite. "You seem to have a penchant for attracting weirdos."

Melanie, who was doing a residency at the large and prestigious County Hospital in her preparation to become a clinical psychologist, said, "Not weirdos, Daddy. They're all just representative of the vast diversity of humanity. Think of them as field research for my career."

"Whatever," Daddy said, "but you'll either live alone or pay for your own vast diversity and field research from now on." His second wife's attorney had extracted a vast amount of money from him without the wonderful anesthetics he used for extraction in his work.

It surprised Daddy to learn that most of these representatives of mankind's diversity didn't love Melanie as much as he did. Some of them, in fact, openly expressed, maybe not hatred, but a bit of contempt. He was astonished that anyone would fail to see Melanie's good qualities. Many of them described her as spoiled. Her own mother, who had left him, had said much the same thing while blaming him for the spoiling.

So Melanie got a nice one-bedroom apartment only blocks from County where she managed to live quite well alone for the first time in her life, for a couple of months anyway, before the inevitable loneliness and fear took over. Then the symptoms returned; first the uneasy feelings, then the full-blown paranoia with the sweating, loss of breath, heart palpitations, and the obsessive checking of doors and windows, the fear of shadows, the fear of noises, the fear of the dark.

The stuff that played nightly in her fertile mind, now crammed full of psychological textbook cases, could have competed with a Stephen King/Tarantino film marathon festival and it seemed to be getting worse with maturity rather than better.

During the course of her studies, she found several categories into which she could conceivably place herself, and some case histories reported in her textbooks that were quite similar to her own experiences and memories. A new fear infiltrated her consciousness, one she had never conceived of before and it was this: Wouldn't it be a hell of a note if she wound up as a case history in a Psych 101 textbook instead of a practicing clinical psychologist which she had been struggling so hard to become all these years?

There was only one thing to do, and that was to get a live-in roommate again so those bizarre textbook symptoms would go away. It had always worked before anyway. Most of the time. Sort of. Okay, it meant a move to larger apartment and probably it meant she would have to get a job unless Daddy relented and still sent money. Really, what's the difference, one bedroom or two, the price would be about the same and she could stay right here in the complex she was in so the move would be inexpensive and easy. The key was to find a reliable, economically stable person who would not stiff her on the rent. Daddy wouldn't even have to know.

The owner/manager of the complex she was living in now was not someone who could be sweet talked into a few days grace either. He was an elderly gentleman with a big round belly, a fringe of white hair around his red bald head and a fiery temper that erupted like Mt. St. Helens on occasion, activating some veins in his big, knobby forehead that turned purple and throbbed ominously. He looked to Melanie like a big, round, fat, ugly mean baby.

He was not a patient man either. His temper tantrums were legendary among his tenants. His name was Leonard L. Leonard.

"My Leonard, he's a good man," Mrs. Leonard would always say, "but patience he doesn't have yet." Evidently she believed there was still a possibility that he could acquire some, though both of them were in their late seventies.

Mrs. Leonard had warned Melanie about her husband the day she moved in. "Pay your rent on time, don't tear stuff up, don't keep animals in the apartment, don't have any loud parties or drunken orgies, park in your designated spot and you'll get on fine with Leonard. And no back talk, of course. He really hates back talk. Especially from women." She grimaced. "I learned that the hard way."

"In other words, just learn to roll over and play dead, is that it then?" Melanie asked.

Mrs. Leonard didn't hear her. She was hard of hearing which was perhaps a defense mechanism she had cultivated during her fifty years of living with Leonard L. Leonard.

Melanie meekly and timidly accepted Mr. Leonard's occasional outbursts. Now she needed to make arrangements to move to another apartment and that required talking to Mr. Leonard.

She chose to go through Mrs. Leonard who would relay the message to her husband. Because Daddy had always faithfully and promptly paid the rent on time, Mrs. Leonard showed her the one empty two-bedroom unit on the ground floor. She made the arrangements for Melanie to move into it at the end of the month. That gave her three weeks to find a new roommate. She had already lined up a part time job doing filing and research for a law firm whose office was near County. The law firm was flexible about her hours, allowing her to work around her schedule at the hospital.

She was ready to embark on a new phase of her life, the first true independence she had ever known. It would be the first time Daddy wasn't paying all the bills.

Of course, there would be the new roommate, but she was going to be very careful in choosing this time.

She had already done a little psychological analysis of all the ex-roommates; a profile delineating the personality traits that led to the end of their association with her, in an attempt to determine what to avoid and what to seek in the new candidate.

She also quite ruthlessly listed her own strengths and weaknesses. On the strength side, she listed loyal, industrious, intelligent, fairly sane and level headed, reliable, neat, generous, fun loving and kind, drug free, studious, thorough, detail oriented, slow to react.

On the weakness side, she listed fearful, even at times paranoid, tendency to binge eating, financial moron, timid, non-assertive, indecisive, slow to react.

So now she thought she knew what she needed in a roommate, above all it had to be someone who was financially reliable and responsible and who had some of the qualities that she, Melanie, lacked, particularly something to counteract that timidity and non-assertiveness that frequently prolonged and intensified her problems.

She put an ad in the university paper that week.

She rejected the wild-eyed little arts major with the piercings and the three-foot dreadlocks because she had no checking account, kept her money in her backpack and tried to live on sales of her paintings.

She rejected the Divinity student whose answer to the question, how much income do you have and how much can you afford to pay for housing? was "That is God's burden, not mine; consider the lilies of the field who neither spin nor toil, yet who are—blah blah and so on. He might well wind up living in a field with those lilies, Melanie decided, unless his faith was very strong, which was okay, quite admirable really, but right now she needed someone with a steady cash flow.

Then Holly came along, Holly with the trust fund from her Grandpa, the real estate king of Agua Blanca, Arizona, Holly with the little red Porsche, Holly with the 5'11" frame, the graceful fall of honey blond hair, the mischievous wide blue eyes and the medals for cross country skiing and running and muscles to match.

Holly was big, brash, bold, rich, confident and assertive. She was exactly what Melanie needed.

Holly promptly and cheerfully paid her share of the rent, utilities and food in advance; she was neat and orderly, she picked up after herself, she liked to cook and she didn't mind cleaning. Her hours were steady and she didn't do drugs, a bit of wine or a six pack now and then but no parties. And best of all, she hit it off with Leonard L. Leonard who was maybe intimidated by her beauty and her youth and her confidence, that sense of authority she possessed and radiated.

Melanie mentioned this to Holly one evening over a plate of spaghetti with homemade sauce that Holly had made while singing songs from a new Adele album.

"Sense of authority? What the hell are you talking about? Of course I'm the final authority on ME, but not much else," she said with a grin.

"That's exactly what I mean," Melanie said.

"You stand up for yourself."

"Well sure. Who else is gonna do it? You see any fairy godmother wandering around here?"

Holly could handle Leonard B. Leonard like he was a mellow little puppy dog. He even fixed the leaky faucet in the bathroom that had probably been leaking for years and he did it cheerfully and quickly, working expertly around his huge belly.

Everybody else in the complex was still asking for their leaky faucets to be fixed.

"I think he's fallen for you or something," Melanie said to Holly.

"Oh, geez, I hope to hell not," Holly said. "Why do you say that?"

"Because I've never seen him so cooperative, so docile, so—so—human."

"Maybe he's on medication, anti-depressants or mood elevators or Viagra or something," Holly said, adding, "God what an appalling thought that last one is."

Holly paid her rent on time, Melanie's job earned her enough to pay her rent on time, so Mr. Leonard was happy and Daddy was happy too. His little girl was growing up and assuming her own financial burdens and her graduate work and residency were also right on track.

Then winter hit, opening with a record-breaking storm. Snow fell steadily for two days and it was driven by a northeast wind screaming down out of Canada and across the freezing lake to batter the city and its residents. When the city was covered with several inches of snow, the storm abruptly ceased and the temperature plunged to 35 degrees below zero in the daytime for three more days.

Streets were closed, schools were closed, traffic slowed to a creeping pace or stopped completely. Cars wouldn't start, buses didn't run. The stark beauty of the snow-covered city was quickly replaced by piles of dirty, soot covered snow as the city snowplows went to work.

Melanie and Holly chose not to attend their classes. The batteries in both their cars were dead and the buses weren't regular when they ran at all. They stayed at home in the still quite cozy apartment wearing several layers of clothing for warmth. Holly made different soups for their meals as they waited the storm out.

On the fifth day of the cold spell, when the snowfall had completely stopped, Holly discovered they had no hot water. There was no cold water either. She checked with the people in the surrounding apartments, most of whom had no water either.

"Some pipes must be frozen," was the consensus. Holly was appointed to inform Leonard L. Leonard. "He gets on well with you," they rationalized.

Holly left a message on his answering machine asking him in her sweetest voice to please drop by to see her.

He showed up a couple of hours later with a heavy plaid cap with ear flaps on his big round head and an oversize orange stuffed nylon parka stretched across his huge belly. His face was red and some drops of snot had frozen at the end of his nose. He wore a heavy pair of black mittens.

Holly quickly explained the problem as she let him into the warmth of their apartment. She left the door open.

"The pipes must be frozen," she said. "And it's like that in B2 and B4 and a couple other units. A lot of us have no water."

"Kuhrist!" he screamed as he jerked the plaid cap off his head revealing the throbbing of the purple veins. "Didn't you people ever hear of letting the faucets drip during a cold snap?" he yelled.

Holly moved to stand in front of him, almost touching his belly, blocking his exit, intimidating him. She had to look down to make eye contact. Melanie cowered in the kitchen.

"Mr. Leonard, most of the faucets here DO drip, summer and winter, night and day," she said firmly, continuing to maintain eye contact.

Mr. Leonard shouted a few more curses at her and she shouted some threats back at him as a couple of people in neighboring units gathered to enjoy the excitement. Mrs. Leonard hurried over with her hair in big rollers covered with a scarf and a long coat over her bathrobe as the shouting match continued.

What happened then seemed to both Holly and Melanie to occur in slow motion, like a scene from an action movie slowed down so the viewers would miss none of the blood and sweat splashing around. Mr. Leonard's puffy, purple face crumpled like a wadded-up tissue, the drop of snot slowly fell off his right nostril and came to rest somewhere on the vast expanse of the orange parka, his eyes rolled up and back into his head as his head jerked spasmodically sideways. His hands in the huge black mittens clutched at his chest.

Holly had time in the slow motion she was suspended in to note that his arms were too short to reach around his belly. She jumped back as he fell forward onto his face, his body hitting the floor with a resounding thud.

She could hear some strangled sounds and then there was silence. She snapped out of the slow-motion trance she was in and rolled his heavy body over as the spectators twittered and milled around them, offering suggestions and advice. Mrs. Leonard let out an ear-splitting screech.

Holly noted that Mr. Leonard's face had turned an even deeper shade of purple, but the veins were ominously still. She yelled for the crowd to give her some room and pounded on his chest a couple of times and someone screamed for someone to call 911 as Mrs. Leonard wailed and clutched at her husband.

Melanie still hung back, watching the action, too frightened to move. The paramedics arrived and wheeled Mr. Leonard off with Mrs. Leonard following as she sniffed and sobbed with her unzipped galoshes slapping and her bathrobe tie trailing on the ice. Melanie sat down on the sofa as the ambulance sped away.

"He'll be all right," Holly said with no conviction as she watched the ambulance drive away through the still open door.

It was several hours later before the word spread through the complex that Mr. Leonard had died of a heart attack. Within a few more days, word spread that those girls in B3 had killed him.

"Those girls?" Melanie said in an outraged tone. "I was ten feet away from him! I didn't say anything! I never touched him!"

"You mean you agree that I killed him?" Holly asked, equally outraged. "All I did was yell at the old asshole! I didn't even touch him either. I may have poked my finger into his big old belly, but that's all!"

"Of course I don't think you killed him," Melanie said in a placating tone.

But Mrs. Leonard and her lawyers thought so. They filed a lawsuit against the tenant in B3, which technically wasn't Holly, whose name wasn't on the lease and who had already seen fit to depart in a major huff even though her rent was paid for three more weeks. Technically and now quite literally, the tenant in B3 was Melanie.

"There's a lawsuit against you?" Daddy screamed when she called him with the news.

Melanie held the receiver away from her ear. It felt hot. Maybe he had melted down a couple hundred miles of cable.

"What in hell for?" Daddy screamed. "What did you do?"

"Nothing, Daddy. I didn't do anything. But the lawyers say I killed my landlord. They think they have a good case," Melanie reported in her timid voice.

"You killed your landlord?" Daddy screamed. "How in hell could you kill your landlord?"

By the time she got to the part of the story about Holly and the frozen pipes, Melanie realized that, lawsuit or no lawsuit, win, lose or draw, this was another turning point in her life, a true rite of passage for her. This would probably be her last roommate.

SEARCH FOR THE KING

For ten generations after the Long Winter, the family of Samuel the Scholar had kept reading and writing alive among the people.

For two hundred years, the People had been too busy scrambling to survive to develop much beyond fire, shelter and a bit of farming, but Samuel longed for more for them. He wanted a religion to give them comfort and hope.

He knew from the books his family had guarded and the oral tradition they had kept alive that the society preceding the Long Winter had had a religion. And he knew that the main symbol of that religion was the star, which was often symbolized by a cross. One such cross he had seen pictured had the inscription The King on it.

It had been Samuel's great grandfather who had discovered the stack of soft cover books that had been Samuel's main source of information on the traditions and religion of the People who had lived before the Long Winter. Samuel knew from these books that they too had called themselves the People. These valuable books had been found in an underground storage space whose walls were of a hard, porous material that helped absorb moisture so the books, in spite of their fragile nature, were quite well preserved.

They were dated and numbered as is proper for Holy Writ. There were beautiful glossy, multi-colored photos of high quality in all of them, but a limited amount of explanatory text which meant that Samuel had to fill in a lot of the blanks in his quest to rediscover the religion of the past. But, he reasoned, isn't that how it had always been done?

Samuel had developed through the years what he thought was a logical and cohesive understanding of the nature of the religion depicted in the books, but he still lacked the main ingredient that would bring it all to life. He had discovered many minor gods and goddesses, but he had not yet discovered the identity of the Head God, the Supreme Deity.

He wanted desperately to find this Head Man, this King, more than he wanted anything else in the world. He wanted it for his People who so badly needed Someone or Something to believe in.

For generations, life had been so difficult and so tenuous that only the very strong had survived, but Samuel could see that even this hardy race who compared themselves to the big, hard-shelled bugs the People ate(fried was best) who survived the Long Winter in the underground wasteland beneath the ruins of the great city, needed something more. They needed the Divine.

There was one such person who appeared occasionally in the soft books who was referred to as Divine, the Divine Miss M as she was called. She always looked very happy so Samuel deduced that happiness must be an aim of this religion. Samuel thought that happiness should be everyone's major goal, but he didn't think this Divine One was the Head Man, mostly because she was a woman.

Not that a woman couldn't be a leader. There were many women leaders in the books, all of them beautiful and often scantily clad goddesses. Still Samuel thought that none of these was the Supreme Leader, none was the King.

There was also one picture in the books of a man called Prince, a young dark man with a guitar. He was wearing a pair of pants with holes cut where the butt cheeks showed through, so Samuel assumed this Prince was a fertility god of some sort. The Prince was handsome and the pants were quite effective. But he obviously wasn't the King.

Samuel waited for and hoped for, and even prayed for more information, enlightenment and understanding so he could pass it on to his People. He was known far and wide as the Scholar, the most learned man among the People who sought his counsel on many things; astronomy, weather, art, science, agriculture, law and morality.

Some even referred to him as the Medicine Man. He desperately needed to find evidence of this Divine One so he could give it to the People, who, like Samuel himself, were longing for something greater than themselves to believe in.

Samuel knew that he would find it. His father had told him that his great grandfather's father's father's favorite saying was, 'seek and you will find', a saying that had been handed down through the generations of his family. This saying had come about because, as bad as the Long Nuclear Winter was, it had solved two of the most pressing problems of those ancient People, the problems of global warming and over population. The seek and you will find must have applied there too. All Samuel knew was that it worked.

So Samuel continued to seek, wandering through the settlements with only the clothes on his back and the soft books in a leather pouch he carried until the snows of winter forced him to seek shelter during the cold months.

He was always welcome among the People who loved to hear the stories from the books. They shared their shelters and their food with him and considered themselves lucky if he wintered in their lodge. They would be entertained by his sharing of the books through the long cold days.

This winter he had chosen to winter with the family of a man who called himself Brad. Brad had taken the name from one of the minor gods who was quite often depicted in the soft books.

That other Brad showed up in the books a lot. He too looked happy. He had a sweet little smile and happy eyes and a big pile of pale colored hair, and he was often shown with women, many different women, all of whom were looking up at him adoringly so Samuel thought he might be a household god of some kind. There were pictures of him surrounded with many children and some of him building houses.

Like the Brad who took his name, Samuel too liked him. Samuel also liked the family of Brad whose shelter was larger and warmer than most. He used the materials he found in creative ways. His home was partially underground and was lined with porous blocks of rock which formed the walls of the shelter above ground too. Large sheets of metal he found in the rubble on the island formed floors and a watertight roof.

Samuel liked staying with Brad. His shelter was warm and Brad knew how to grow corn and beans so there was always food; dried stone ground corn which made a delicious mush when cooked with water and it made good flat cakes of bread too. Brad learned how to dry the greens he would find and collect in the spring too so the diet of his family was good. And in summer, when the corn was cooked fresh, it was the most wonderful dish of all, fit for the gods.

Most of all, Samuel loved to visit the huge broken statue that Brad's sons had discovered on the shore of the island a few summers ago. The head was broken off the body which lay in three more pieces, but the noble face with the fine, barely smiling, slightly curled upper lip, was intact. Part of an inscription remained too. "Give me your tired, your poor, your huddled masses yearning to breathe free" it said.

Samuel pondered that inscription for a long time. That was surely a description of his own People. He became more and more certain this gigantic statue was of the Main Deity, the King he was seeking.

Samuel often arranged his travels to allow him to spend time with Brad and his large family so he could contemplate the words on the statue and the face, longing and praying for the complete revelation to come to him.

And then his prayers were answered. One chill morning, Brad stood before him with his arms extended. And there it was. Another one of the soft books, this one ragged and torn, but the title, People, was still there. And inside, just as always, the minor gods and goddesses were called Stars. Some, especially, the ones called Rock Stars, wore representations of the Star, the cross.

On the cover was a large photo of a person whose face looked like a living version of the face of the statue. He was beautiful, with sleek dark hair as black as the raven's wing and fine, pale skin. He wore a beautiful smile and the lip curled just like the lip on the gigantic statue.

He wore a flowing white cape spangled with sparkly stars and many strands of gold chains. Under the photo was a caption that read "The King Returns."

Samuel was shaking with excitement. The King Returns. He had found what he had been seeking, the knowledge that was undoubtedly the cornerstone of this ancient faith that he would make new and give to his People.

Inside the book, there was more evidence. This man, it said, had made more money thirty years after his reported death than anybody else ever had. In addition to that, fifty thousand people worldwide, (worldwide? So it was a worldwide religion, Samuel realized with delight) made their living impersonating him. Very good for a dead man, Samuel thought, but wait, maybe he wasn't dead at all. Wasn't that what Head Boss Gods always did, come back from the dead? This God was reportedly seen everywhere, at malls which Samuel thought, quite rightly were a huge bunch of stores that sold all sorts of stuff, on the streets, in churches, on mountaintops, in the deserts, in the Halls of Government. There were photos of Him bending down to kiss his adoring disciples who were so obviously moved that Samuel was sure this was the Main God.

And best of all, there were photos and reports of a temple called Graceland dedicated to the Caped King in a place called Memphis. It was reported that millions of people every year made pilgrimages to this Holy Shrine.

Samuel was so excited he could barely breathe. He had seen references to this temple in other sacred texts, although not in the inspired texts of the People books. And yes, there it was, the final holy piece of information that would make his understanding complete so that he could build a comprehensive religion for his People. His Name. His Holy Name. It was Elvis. Samuel could not wait to share this Great News with his People.

UNCLE EDDIE'S PLANE TRIP

I was twisting and turning in my sleep, my new red and black flowered satin pajamas so slick on the sheets that it woke me up.

I had been dreaming of Uncle Eddie in some tropical place with palm trees and flowering vines and sunshine, Uncle Eddie in shorts and sandals. I wish we knew where he was. His usual uniform here on the ranch was a pair of bib overalls and high-top lace-up black work shoes, not shorts and sandals. He would have made fun of any man wearing such a ridiculous outfit.

Uncle Eddie was my grandmother's brother and he was already old by the time I knew him. He was always my favorite uncle. It wasn't just because he always had those butterscotch candies wrapped in gold cellophane in the pocket of his bib overalls either. He liked kids. My cousins liked him too. And we were his great nieces and nephews, the second generation to be given the candy so he had enough real experience with kids to know about them.

It wasn't just sentimentality like Grandma and Aunt Ellen suspected his romantic streak was. That came from long ago when he was young and the girl he was going to marry, Alice, got bit by a rattlesnake just weeks before the wedding and died. His grief was so overwhelming that he took the train from the home place in Nebraska to northern Wyoming where his two sisters, Grandma and Aunt Ellen, lived with their husbands and families.

"He enshrined the dead Alice in his heart and never looked at another woman," Aunt Ellen told me one time. "And that left me and your Grandma to do everything for him for the rest of his life."

"And if I remember right," Grandma added with a grin, "That Alice wasn't much of a looker."

"A great talker though," Aunt Ellen said.

I don't know if Alice was a great talker, but I knew that Uncle Eddie was. He never tired of telling us all about the incomparable Alice.

And it was true that Grandma and Aunt Ellen fed and housed and washed and cleaned for him. In addition to taking care of him, it seemed to me that they tried to run him too. Although it was pretty much of an impossibility. He was one of those ornery old timers up there in that northern part of Wyoming, one of those independent types who thought they invented everything from running cattle to farming. Uncle Eddie even thought he invented thinking and took great pains to let us kids know how well his head worked and he knew nobody could do anything right except him. I think he also thought he invented sex, but I later figured out he didn't. My generation did that. I sure understood why Grandma and Aunt Ellen got upset with him. But I loved him anyway.

"He's the reason the words cantankerous and curmudgeon were thought up," Grandma said.

"Not to mention crabby, grouchy, grumpy and sorehead," Aunt Ellen added.

Aunt Ellen and Grandma and I were sitting on the summer porch one hot summer day, shelling peas from Grandma's huge garden with Uncle Eddie supervising. He was rhapsodizing as usual about the lost Alice when Grandma asked him to please make himself useful and bring the pitcher of iced tea from the refrigerator. He went off for the tea mumbling and grumbling.

"Maybe it will keep him busy so he won't talk about her," Aunt Ellen whispered with a grin.

"Probably only death will end that line of talk about her," Grandma whispered back. She was grinning too.

I was sixteen that summer and susceptible to that sort of thing. "I think it's sweet and romantic," I said.

Aunt Ellen snorted. "Sweet? Romantic? Wait until you've heard it for forty years straight. It's vomit inducing."

Grandma nodded. "If that rattlesnake hadn't bit poor Alice and if she had lived to marry him, the romance would have died a natural death due to the often toxic effect of matrimony."

"No," Aunt Ellen said. "It wouldn't have been a natural death. Edward himself would have killed the romance. With his disagreeable disposition and demanding ways."

They both laughed.

"I know he's ornery," I said, "but I still think it's romantic."

"You're sixteen and single," Grandma said. "Just wait."

Uncle Eddie must have heard us because he put the pitcher of tea down and announced that he was going fishing. "You can get your own glasses," he added in a haughty tone.

Later that evening, I heard Grandma and Uncle Eddie arguing over who should gut and clean the fish he had caught. He was a great hunter who would bring home white tail deer and antelope, sage hens and grouse, and an occasional porcupine or muskrat or prairie dog or raccoon. Sometimes he brought home some frog legs he got with his .22 rifle and often he would bring home the ugly, black, boney, muddy tasting bullheads from the reservoirs near the ranch. Once he even brought home a black bear that had been terrorizing his best friend Sander Ewing's herd of registered sheep up in the gumbo flats beyond the pine hills near the Montana border. Grandma and Aunt Ellen cooked it all up and said they were glad to get it.

As a kid, it seemed to me that Uncle Eddie could do anything. When I learned the term in school, I mentioned to Grandma that he was a regular renaissance man.

"Maybe," she agreed. "If those renaissance men were all unemployed bachelors living off relatives."

"More like unemployable," Aunt Ellen added. "And if sitting on the couch and complaining and bitching about how we do his laundry and cook and thinking up ways to fix the government are what makes a renaissance man, then he's it all right. And don't forget about being ornery as an old wet hen."

Joyce Keveren

There were a lot of things about Uncle Eddie that pissed Grandma and Aunt Ellen off, like how he hit four oil wells on his land while they hit only 4 together, and he still didn't buy any groceries or give them any money for bills, but the thing that pissed them off the most was his irrational fear of flying. "For a man who thinks he can do anything and claims to be afraid of nothing, it is just plain odd," Aunt Ellen said.

It was odd, especially considering that he helped his best friend, Sander Ewing, rebuild a small old single engine airplane. Uncle Eddie was a great mechanic too. He kept Grandpa's cars and trucks and tractors running.

Sander flew that little plane all over the country and he always asked Uncle Eddie to ride along.

"I ain't getting in that thing," Uncle Eddie pronounced. "Not ever."

"You're scared then?" Aunt Ellen asked.

"You might say that," Uncle Eddie growled.

"I did say that," Aunt Ellen said.

"Well, I call it just plain smart," Uncle Eddie said. "I see it like this. If your fuel pump goes out on a car or truck, or the alternator or water pump goes, you can pull her over to the side of the road and get out. Still alive. If something goes wrong in a plane, try stepping out alive. No, sir, I don't fly."

It made sense to me. I was always hearing about all those small plane crashes. Uncle Eddie had long ago convinced me of his superior ability to think and reason things out. And when Sander Ewing was killed in a fiery crash of his little plane, it only reinforced Uncle Eddie's determination not to fly.

By the 1960's, Aunt Ellen's and Grandma's kids had all scattered around the country, but they were a close-knit group and they visited each other often, for holidays and other events, like graduations and weddings and a burial here and there. Grandma and Aunt Ellen would fly to Portland where Aunt Ellen's oldest daughter and her family lived or to Phoenix where Grandma's son's family lived or back to Nebraska where their sister's large family still lived.

Uncle Eddie would sometimes take a train or a bus if it was a special occasion like the 50th wedding anniversary of his sister in Nebraska, but he steadfastly refused to fly.

"You won't ever get me on a plane," he said in his most stubborn voice.

"The big jets have more than one engine, Edward," Aunt Ellen pointed out one time when she was packing for a trip to Portland.

"They still crash," Uncle Eddie responded.

"Statistics say you are more apt to die of a lightning strike than in a plane crash," Grandma said. She was terrified of the lightning strikes there on the high plains and I think she made that up.

"That may well be the truth, but tell it to Sander. It is true for me because I will never go anywhere for anything in any kind of airplane."

"Don't be so sure, Edward. You may know everything there is to know, but you are not God," Aunt Ellen pronounced. "And you do not know what is going to happen."

"You're just too stubborn," Grandma said. "And out of date. You talked yourself into that corner and now you're just too stubborn to change or admit you're wrong."

"Could be," Uncle Eddie agreed. "But I won't get on a plane."

"If God had wanted you to fly, he would have given you wings. Is that it, Edward?" Aunt Ellen said. She was particularly pissed at him because he was choosing to miss her granddaughter's wedding in Portland, a hasty affair that had been brought about most likely due to a pre-nuptial pregnancy, which was an established tradition in our family. Of course that tradition died when some of the younger ones, girls mostly, decided to bypass marriage altogether. The speed of the decision to do the wedding had made a bus trip impossible for Uncle Eddie.

"And she was your favorite niece, too," she said in an aggravated tone.

"She still is," Uncle Eddie said with a nod toward me. "You're the favorite grandniece," he told me. He turned back to Aunt Ellen. "And it's got nothing to do with wings and God. It's just common sense. I won't fly. And speaking of God since you dragged him into this, God invented soap operas so you have to watch them? Is that it? Day after day?"

I could tell by the set of her jaw and the fire in her eye that this wasn't over for Aunt Ellen.

Joyce Keveren

Several years later, Aunt Ellen moved to Portland to be near her daughter and to get away from the harsh winters in Wyoming after the death of her husband.

Her 85th birthday was coming up and shortly after hers, Uncle Eddie's 87th, so a big celebration was being planned with all the scattered members of the family.

Uncle Eddie got all spruced up, bought a new suit and took the bus to Portland where he enjoyed his trips to the beach so much that he decided to stay on an extra couple of weeks after everyone else went home.

He was in the back yard on a warm summer afternoon picking blackberries off the vine on the back fence, eating them as he picked them when he had a heart attack and cried out for help. Aunt Ellen heard him from the back deck and called the paramedics but he died on the way to the hospital.

Grandma said Aunt Ellen was barely coherent when she first called to deliver the news. When Grandma hung up the phone, she was crying. "Your Uncle Edward is gone," she told me. She put her arms around me and we cried together for a bit.

"Now," she said. "We have things to do."

She dug out the old tin box in the back of her closet where all the family's important papers were stored; the birth certificates, wills, titles and deeds, division orders and lease agreements from the oil and gas leases, and a few letters printed in pencil from her little grandchildren that were precious to her too.

She called Aunt Ellen back to tell her that she had found Uncle Eddie's will and his instructions in the event of his death. I listened to the phone call.

"He appointed me executor. I have to pay all the bills for the last things. He says he wants to be cremated and his ashes buried here at home in the community cemetery. So I think it's best that you arrange for his cremation there don't you think? Now stop crying, Ellen, and listen. He left all the money that's left from the land leases and the oil and gas leases to his nieces and grandnieces. Quite a lot from the looks of that last bank statement." There was a pause. "No, none to the boys."

Grandma held the phone away from her ear and grinned at me. I could hear Aunt Ellen yelling.

"Yes," Grandma said when Aunt Ellen finally hushed. "It's just exactly what he would do in memory of old Alice. Edward the incurable romantic. But it was his decision to make. Just put those ashes on a bus home and we'll take care of it."

I could hear Aunt Ellen yelling again.

"Don't do that Ellen," Grandma said. "You know how he hated the thought of flying."

They argued a bit more and finally Grandma said, "I'll mail you a check for the money for the expenses." She sighed and hung up the phone.

"I just know she's going to put him on a plane just to prove him wrong. Even if he's dead, he won't like that."

"But it won't matter, will it?" I said.

"I'm not sure what the dead know and don't know," Grandma said. "But in any case, there is nothing we can do now."

"It won't matter," I said to comfort her although I had no idea what the dead want either, even though I suspected it might be pretty much what they wanted before they died which in that case meant he did not want to go on a damn plane.

Boy was I wrong that it didn't matter. Aunt Ellen sure enough put Uncle Eddie's ashes on a plane. She even took a taxi to the airport and did it herself, then called Grandma to tell her when to pick them up. We drove the 60 miles into town to the little airport on the right day, but there was no package.

Aunt Ellen had the airlines try to trace the package and they had to admit it was lost.

Uncle Eddie was lost. Just as he had always thought, he should never have got on a plane.

Three months went by with Aunt Ellen reporting the exchanges between her and the airline while Grandma fretted and worried.

"That airline offered money," Aunt Ellen said. "MONEY!" She was outraged. "I told them there are things that money can't fix and this is sure one of them. That package contained my brother's ashes."

"We're not suers," Grandma said, but Aunt Ellen must have threatened a law suit because the airline kept looking.

Finally Aunt Ellen called to say they had found him. My dream was right. He was in the lost and found room at the airport in Miami with the palm trees and the sunshine of my dream.

Aunt Ellen wasn't the least bit remorseful about putting him on an airplane and when she showed up for the burial service at home, she and Grandma saw to it that he was buried where he wanted to be. When we got home from the cemetery, they both cried and cried until they started to laugh.

"Stubborn old goat," Aunt Ellen said. "He was wrong. An airplane ride wouldn't have killed him. I was right."

"It couldn't kill him, Ellen," Grandma pointed out. "He was already dead, but they LOST him, and you know he wouldn't have liked that much either. So he was right too."

I fell asleep listening to them and dreamed of Uncle Eddie. He was out on the prairie watching a rattlesnake glide away from him with lightening all along the sky line while a lovely girl in a white dress walked toward him. It had to be Alice even though this girl was not homely. I hope this dream is true too.

JUSTICE FOR MARK

I met Mark the day the prison guard shoved him roughly into my cell. He looked stunned, like a steer at the stockyards that had been hit in the head with a hammer, his eyes big and scared with heavy dark circles around them. He was skinny and raw looking and appeared barely able to stand.

I said hello and pointed to the bunk over my head.

"You look like a dying calf in a hailstorm," I said with a grin, a saying I had picked up in Wyoming ranch country just before I got busted for DUI the fourth and final time that landed me in this gray cement holding pen in Iowa, my home state.

"I'm Pete Hardin," I told him and I made him welcome. He looked like he didn't have a friend in the world, like he's never had a friend in fact.

I had figured out, after six months of forced sobriety, that there was another side to me besides that drunken dickhead who got thrown in here. Those MADD women were right; drunk driving is bad. BADD. I should start a group called BADD. Badasses Against Drunk Driving. Anyway, I figured this out after only four incarcerations: I could be a decent guy when I was sober and it never hurts to be kind.

In the next few weeks, I learned some things about my new cell mate too. I learned he had a huge crush on Serena Williams, that Amazon woman of steel I'd hate to meet in a dark alley somewhere when she was pissed at me, a woman so brave and tough she could win a top-level tennis tournament while seven months pregnant. I could sure understand Mark's infatuation for this woman, but she would make two of him. Her hair was bigger than him. But love is hard to figure. I myself had once married a sweet little blond Sunday school teacher who, it turned out, could hate like Hitler when provoked. And I sure provoked her. Not with anything in particular that I could see, but just by being me.

I had pretty much provoked that disreputable pack of bullies in here too, especially the leader, that pot-bellied, pock-marked slacker with the bad liver. I ignored him as long as I could, but he finally pushed his fat finger in my chest, so I did one of my modified wrestling take-downs on him and he hit the ground, big belly, damaged liver and all. I used to be a pretty good wrestler when I was younger and I still use the gym equipment in here to stay in shape. When he finally managed to stagger to his feet, I looked down at him, right in his yellowed eyes and told him I'd had enough. Turns out his collarbone got broken and he wore a sling for a couple of weeks all the while glaring at me through those little yellow eyes, but nobody ever said a word to me about the fight.

When I started taking care of Mark, the bully and his pack of followers tried to start up with their meanness again, but they soon tired of the game and backed off. I guess their memory about the broken collar bone was pretty good.

They snickered and talked about my new 'woman', but I didn't care and told Mark to ignore them. I would be out of here long before Mark was, but I figured he could learn to take care of himself before that happened.

"What are you in for?" I asked him one night after lights out.

"Murder," he said after a long pause.

Now that surprised me so I shut up. The fact is that Mark looked and acted less like a murderer than anyone I could think of. He looked like one of those dying English poet types to me, the ones my little sister used to love, with his lank brown hair and pale skin with those blue veins showing through and those deep, dark eyes with the long lashes. His whole body was frail as a dried out sunflower stalk that would be blown to bits in a high wind. Not your usual TV type murderer. And there was all that reading and writing too. But you never know what anyone is capable of.

Another thing I learned from the counselors and AA and the Higher Power which I had pretty much always underestimated was that it is good to talk about things, especially the deep, dark, hidden things, the shameful things. You have to acknowledge the inner crap before you can even start to fix it. And there isn't anything, to my way of thinking, that can't be fixed, in spite of what those preachers say about unforgiveable sins. I'm going to remember to tell Mark that. More than once. He sure needs to hear that. I think the word sin should be taken out of the dictionary first thing, and out of the Bible too, because of all the bad ideas us sinners have stored in our heads. Replace that word SIN with mistake maybe or screw-up. Fuckup would be even better. There's no hellfire and no smell of brimstone around that word.

I had also learned that Mark had been to college too. He was an educated dude and a lover of literature and poetry. He was also a killer, but it seemed to me that was less by design and more by accident. The poetry lover was dominant, in my mind at least.

I dropped the subject of killing and asked,

"How did you get the name Mark? Family name?"

You have to understand my interest in names comes to me naturally. With a name like Peter Hardin, which the school kids I knew growing up always changed to Peter Hard-on, it was bound to happen. I questioned my parents' sanity and brain power for years. But one good thing, young Peter Hard-On learned early on how to handle bullies.

I thought about his name, Mark Justis and wondered why a bright guy like him didn't go on to be a lawyer. Seems logical to me in the same way that gold medal winning Chinese swimmer was named He She Win, or that Detroit Tigers infielder was named Prince Fielder. Or a dickhead like I was got a name like Peter Hardin.

He said no, it wasn't a family name. And he said it wasn't from the Matthew, Mark, Luke and John quartet either.

"My dad's name was Abe," he said. "Like that Old Testament patriarch, Abraham who was so willing to sacrifice his own son."

It sounded to me like he thought his dad was capable of that too.

"My mother was—is a teacher," he went on, "and her favorite writer was Mark Twain. Our family farm was less than a marathon's distance from the Mississippi River, but I wasn't named for him either."

"Maybe the name is from all that writing you do," I asked. "Making your mark?"

He grinned and his whole face lightened. "More like from a mark, a blemish, a spot, an imperfection."

"It's a good name."

"I remember my dad always saying whenever I displeased him which was often, 'Mark my words, that boy is headed for trouble.' And my mom would say that I would do great things. Turns out the old man was right. Trouble sure hit the road to meet me," he said.

"There's still time for your mom to be right too," I told him.

Then one day when we were ready for sleep after lights out, I finally asked him, "So who'd you kill?"

"You don't want to know," he mumbled.

"Yeah, I do or I wouldn't have asked," I said. He must have known by then that was true. I don't just blabber. I mean what I say. I may not have his learning or vocabulary, but I say what I mean.

"Okay," he said. "My dad. I killed my dad."

I left it there for that night, but gradually the whole story came out of him, a bit at a time like drops of acid leaking out of a defective battery. Or maybe he saw me as a Civil War surgeon hacking bits of gangrenous flesh off his damaged body. Like some of those counselors I had.

I changed the subject. "What are you writing?" I asked.

"Poetry," he said.

I thought that was a good thing even though I had never read much poetry and had sure never written any although for a short time when I was in love with the Sunday school teacher who turned on me, I had thought about it.

He told me about his love for the thirteenth century Persian poet Rumi and he read me some of his favorite passages from his book of Rumi's translated works.

It turned out this Rumi had played a part in Mark's story of how he had wound up in this prison too.

He told me how he had abandoned his Midwest Protestant religion when he studied Buddhism in college, told me how he then abandoned the Buddha when he heard about Rumi. Mark thought that Rumi was like John Lennon and pretty much wanted to do away with the established religions.

"Not a bad idea on the whole," I told him. "I would like to hear more from this Rumi."

Mark said he dropped out of college with only about 30 hours to a degree in secondary education. He told his mother and he said he could see that she was disappointed. So he asked her what he could possibly teach anyone. Because he didn't know anything. Of course, he admitted that he was just a kid so he thought he knew everything too, a contradiction that didn't even register then.

"My dad was yelling that you don't have to know anything to be a teacher. Look at your mother. And he was laughing at his own awful joke while I could see my mom, the teacher, just seething with an inner rage. She had told me once she knew one savage thing and that was that the bruises of physical abuse which the old man dished out too, healed more quickly than the constant jabs of verbal battering.

"And Dad was yelling something about marking his words, I'll be supporting that boy forever while my mom was muttering about how she was the one supporting HIM with her teaching because the goddamn farm hadn't made a dime in years and wouldn't ever make any money, since the old man was a lazy slob. And that was true too. And I'm in the middle of it, the cause of it all.

"Then my mom asked me to go chop some wood even though there was a pile already chopped on the porch I had done earlier in the fall. She was just trying to protect me like always from the wrath of the old man.

"A winter storm was moving in and a heavy snow had started to fall. It was Thanksgiving vacation and my mom was cooking a turkey. I chopped wood for an hour or so and brought some in and stacked them by the fireplace.

"After we ate, I sat with Mom at the little table near the fireplace where she graded papers. I told her about Rumi, how his family had moved from Afghanistan which was part of the Persian Empire back then, to escape the Mongol armies in the 13th century. They moved to Turkey where he became a sheikh of the Dervish community and wrote poetry. I showed her my pictures of modern-day dervishes in their long white skirts whirling in ecstasy. She told me I used to do that when I was little, only without the white skirt of course. I read her some of my favorite pieces of Rumi's poetry and she liked it too.

"We thought my dad had fallen asleep with his stomach too full of turkey and dressing, but he reared up in his chair and yelled, 'Rhuemy? Like rheumatism? What the hell kind of name is that?' And he glowered at us and kept muttering.

"When he settled down again, I told my mom I wanted to visit Turkey. I wanted to fly to Istanbul and see Rumi's homeland for myself. We talked about it for a while and I promised her I would go back and finish my degree after the trip to Turkey.

"I told her what the flight would cost and she wrote a check saying it would be an early Christmas present. She said she wished she could go with me.

"The snow was still falling and the sun was going down so it was getting dark and colder as she wrote the check."

I heard something in his voice and I knew there was bad news coming. I mumbled something about how she was a good mother to do that.

He paused for a moment and then he went on. "And then my vision of Istanbul faded when I saw my dad lunge from his chair and grab the check from her hand and throw it in the fire, all the while yelling and screaming. I saw him hit her, first across the face with the flat of his hand and then he doubled his fists up. Even now when I see him in my mind, I see him with his fists doubled up and his arms hanging at his sides, all stiff with rage."

Mark swallowed hard and I could hear him shift around on the top bunk. He cleared his throat.

"So I picked up one of those fifteen inch pieces of hard oak I had chopped and I hit him in the back of the head. Twice. Or maybe even three times. To stop him from hitting Mom. And he went down."

"You killed him?" I asked.

He said, "Yeah, I thought so. Then I dropped the stick of wood and stumbled to the bathroom and shut the door and threw up until I was empty.

"I heard my mother screaming and screaming, saying over and over, you killed him, you killed him, you killed him. And his complaints had stopped."

I could see the snow falling that Thanksgiving Day as he described it and I could see his father lying in a pool of his blood. I could hear the anguish in Mark's voice.

"I washed my face and hands and cleaned up the vomit and went out to my mom. She was still screaming and crying. I threw that bloody piece of wood into the fire. Blood was still running out of the wound in his head and there was a big pool of it on the floor. Mom called the sheriff. She said we needed a lawyer and an undertaker too."

He jumped off the top bunk and looked at me and the sadness was so strong on his face that I wanted to cry or hug him or both.

"And that's how I got here."

I nodded. "Manslaughter?" I knew he only got 12 years with parole possible in 10 so it must have been manslaughter.

He nodded and drew a deep breath. "That's about as bad as it gets."

"I've heard worse. You were protecting your mother. She said you would do something great. Maybe this was it."

"No. I KILLED my father, Pete. I killed him."

"But it's okay," I said, for all the world like I knew a damn thing about stuff like that. In my head I could hear that preacher from back home bellowing about sin and its wages. I ignored the old jerk just like always. "It's okay," I repeated. "There ain't nothing that can't be fixed."

He was silent for a moment like maybe he was thinking about it. I could hear him shifting around up there. Finally, he said, "Now my mom's lost the farm and she's moved into town. I think that's what she wanted to do. I sort of wanted to keep the land and try to farm it someday," he said wistfully. "Without the old man there yelling of course."

"I know what you mean," I told him. "My mom's keeping our family farm going now after my dad died, leasing out the farmland so I can run it when I get out of here," I told Mark. "You can come there when you get out. Live with me. Start over."

Later, after I met his mother on visitor's day, I thought that walloping his father would have been exactly what she considered a good thing. But there was something just a bit off about her. Something missing. Something I couldn't quite figure out.

I could see there had to be more to Mark's story, but I didn't know what. There was something that didn't quite add up. I knew that Mark wasn't one of those congenital liars, but I wasn't so sure about his mother.

Shortly after Mark told me how he had killed his father, he began to have severe stomach pains.

At first I thought he was faking it, but they always took him to the infirmary and did tests and tried to help him. And they gave him pain pills. But the doctors never found anything wrong physically. So they turned him over to the prison shrink who said he was filled with guilt and sorrow so strong it could make him sick.

I believed that. It was making me a bit queasy too.

About a year later, he died in his sleep. Just like that. The night before, he had given me his most prized possession, his copy of the poetry of Rumi. I should have known then that he was planning suicide. One of those counselors had told me that giving your stuff away was a sure-fire sign of suicide plans.

They discovered pain killers in his system. Enough to kill him. He had somehow stashed enough Percocet and oxycontin or whatever else he used to kill himself. Or maybe he had bought it through the inside dealers. That was easy enough to do.

His mother came to see me sometime after his funeral. She said she had come to pick up his few possessions and decided to stop in to see me. She was wearing a nice-looking suit and her hair was cut short and I'm pretty sure dyed and she looked pretty good for a woman her age, which I figured was almost old enough to be my mother.

"I flew to Istanbul to scatter his ashes," she said. "Since he had never been able to go there and he wanted to so bad." She was crying.

I tried to comfort her by telling her what I knew about Mark and how much I had liked him. "He told me about that Thanksgiving Day," I said. "How he was trying to protect you."

Her crying stopped abruptly and her eyes narrowed and her face sort of closed down. "What did he tell you?" It came out more like a threat than a question.

I knew the woman was hiding something so I decided to bluff. I'm a pretty good poker player. "He told me everything. He knew everything."

A startled look crossed her face so I took another gamble. "He knew what you did."

"He saw it?" she asked. There was a note of panic in her voice.

I nodded. "He said he saw it." I had no idea what I was talking about.

But she did. "What're you going to do about it?" She spat the words at me.

I looked at her, a long stare that I hoped was intimidating. "Nothing," I said. "It's over. Mark's gone. His dad's gone," I added.

"And good riddance," she said in a fierce tone.

"Yes," I agreed. "Mark told me how mean he was. Said he had it coming."

"He did. I was protecting Mark too."

How were you protecting Mark I wondered.

Then I knew. Her face registered the change on mine.

"Yes, that's right. While Mark was throwing up, the old bastard tried to get up, struggled to his knees. So I picked up that bloody piece of wood Mark had used and I hit him some more. I finished him off. I was screaming bloody murder all the while."

"Literally," I mumbled.

"Mark came out of the bathroom and threw the bloody piece of wood into the fire, the evidence, and we both calmed down and I called the sheriff. Mark told him he did it. Well, he did some of it, didn't he? I was thinking that I would never tell anyone what I had done; not the sheriff, not Mark, not God, not even myself." She gave me appraising look. "I don't know why I'm telling you. But Mark was younger than me, and a man and he would survive prison better than me wouldn't he?" she said belligerently.

I didn't know why she was telling me either, other than she needed to unload it. If you are polite enough to listen to people, they often unload on you. "You know I cared about Mark, don't you?" I said.

"I just let Mark tell that sheriff that he did it.

I had to work, didn't I? So there would be a place for Mark when he got out of here?"

She was as belligerent as one of the old brood sows my dad kept on the farm. Some of them would eat their young when they were crazy enough.

Just how much meanness can a human take before they go crazy and get mean too? I felt a bit of pity for her then. Not much, but a bit. I wished that what I had said was true, I wished that Mark had known what she had done so he would have lived. The bit of pity left me then with no farewell and not a trace lingered.

I asked her to leave. "Don't worry. I'll keep your awful secret. Just go. I will forget you."

I hoped that was true. I wanted to forget her. I know I've forgotten a lot of people. I don't know who they are since I forgot them, but I sure want to forget her. Of course that may never happen because I know I will never forget Mark.

She will pay somehow. There is justice in the Divine scheme of things. There has to be because there is so often no justice here. I got out his book of Rumi's poetry and looked for something to console me. Mark said there was stuff in there for every situation and I thought about Mark speaking of his parents, Abe named for the Biblical Abraham and that cold crazed woman who had just left. It seemed odd to me, but she was the one who was most like the old Abraham, patriarch of the Bible because not only had she been willing to sacrifice her son, she had actually done it.

THE RED LIMOUSINE

Idio Sauvan, my yoga/meditation teacher, had been yapping for months about how the Universe works, how the inexorable law of cause and effect operates impartially for all times, all peoples, all places. No exceptions. No reprieves. No last-minute call from the Governor. Maybe a rain check now and then, but you will get what you give. All in all, I approved of the theory. It's as fair a system as could be developed by God or Anybody Else.

And, Idio said, the law of magnetism/attraction brings you what you want too, or in the paraphrased words of another great teacher, fill out a requisition form and you will get a delivery. There again, no exceptions, no exemptions; a delay perhaps, an alternate form maybe since the Universe is in a constant state of flux, but you will get what you want. And remember too, you get what you give so be careful what you give.

Idio counseled his student to pay strict attention with unrelenting vigilance to their thoughts and their lives which were, he said, one and the same thing. We were told to observe the flow of life itself so we could chart and verify the phenomena of cause/effect and attraction/magnetism in our own lives.

In the midst of observing and charting, I met Daniel even though I could not recall ever having asked for him. As a single straight woman nearing thirty, I had, of course, asked for a man, a lot of men even, but I think not in that particular package. "You must be specific!" Idio always said, throwing the blame right back to me, where, of course, it rightfully belonged.

As a matter of fact, it was Idio who introduced me to Daniel at the Goat Hide Café, the current "In" watering hole for the vegetarian crowd; a tacky, vine-covered shack in a cluttered alley advertised as Third World Chic where a plate of lentils garnished with a sprig of cilantro sold for fifteen bucks.

It was a point of pride with Daniel, I was soon to learn, that he pay exorbitant sums of money for attractions of dubious worth that were currently "In".

Daniel was a perfect example of the 21st century man, handsome, well dressed, blow dried, with an air of money, taste and distinction, a man who would look good on TV, a man much like our contemporary politicians. Never mind that the image was a felonious façade that covered a festering plethora of psychological problems. But that too was "In".

I can hear you asking how a dedicated student of the brilliant and lauded Idio Sauvan, teacher of yoga and metaphysics, could fall for a shallow, half-toned person like Daniel. It's simple. I was in love, deep, blinding, unbending love. I would not know the depths of Daniel's shallowness until later, much later when the rosy-hued aura of that love exploded into a fiery red funeral revelation, and, of course, there was the sex. I admit it.

Idio often said that sex is the supreme expression of divine love on this planet, a metaphysical manifestation of the unification of the Paradox of Being. One time he even said that sex was the epitome of the Divine Joke, that joke that tied procreation to sex. Whatever, it was damn good sex. And I do remember having asked often, and quite specifically for that very thing: some good sex at some point in my life before I died.

Daniel's psychological problems were myriad, but the big one, he said, was his father.

In those early deformative years of his life, Daddy was an agent of the DEA, the Drug Enforcement Agency and Daniel was a teenager, non-resistant to peer pressure, experimenting with the Big Three Joys/Vices of Life in the late 20th century; sex, drugs and rock and roll.

He played in a garage band called Prickz in Heat, grew some pathetic dreadlocks, smoked, snorted and ingested a wide variety of controlled substances while trying to grow to manhood under the roof of a narc; a calamity, he said, that warped his fragile psyche, leaving him unalterably scarred forever.

After hundreds of hours and thousands of dollars of therapy, not to mention medication, uncontrolled this time, all paid for inadvertently by the DEA, Daniel had become well enough to seek a job and live on his own. Except, of course, Dad still paid most of his bills out of his old narc retirement fund, as Daniel's career of choice, marketing engineer, although it paid well, did not cover his taste for the luxurious.

Daniel was well enough to visit his Dad occasionally, but only after indulging in a ritual that he had worked out in his head, a ritual that involved a vision of his father's funeral.

"I'm going to rent a red limousine when that bastard dies and drive all around the city drinking champagne and shouting, 'Freedom! Freedom! I'm free! I'm free at last!'"

Actually he told everybody that. Often.

I met Rudolf, his dad at a family Christmas gathering where all the relatives got gloriously drunk on a bottle of something I think they called Gutzrotsk which tasted like coal oil smells and indeed had been used to start fires in the Old Country, which I gathered was somewhere between Little Rock, Arkansas and Siberia, Russia. It was between a rock and a hard place anyway.

Rudolf was a distinguished, silver haired old gentleman with erect carriage, soft southern speech and a ready smile that lit his brown eyes and spilled over to warm me.

"I do a combover to hide the horns and tuck the tail under my jacket," he whispered as we shook hands. I guess he knew about Daniel's ritual too.

"Daniel has told me so much about you," I stammered as the Gutzrotsk ate into my stomach lining.

Thinking that dumb response would end our relationship right there before it began, I started to slink off when his laughter stopped me. We were friends from that moment on.

Though I still listened to Daniel's horror stories from his childhood, both before and after the death of his mother, I could no more place the Rudolf I knew in the plays that were produced in Daniel's head than I could cast myself as Mother Teresa, but the sex was still good.

"Okay, Daniel, your pain is real. Or it WAS real. I'll concede that," I told him. "I can feel it. But it's not mine and it's over. I like your Dad. He's good to me."

The truth was: I was falling in love with Rudolf at about the same rate I was falling out of love with Daniel. An equal and opposite reaction as Idio would say, conforming to the laws of physics which in reality, Idio said, were also the laws of metaphysics, one and the same. Never mind that my confused feelings were irrational and that Rudolf was 89 years old to my thirty. And the father of my lover. He was kind, considerate, funny and charming. He bought real dinners for me; Mongolian Beef Barbecue, Mama's Southern Fried Chicken, Chico's Tacos, McDonald's hamburgers, whatever I craved.

"This reminds me of the depression years in the hard winters of '38 and '39 back in the Old Country," Rudolf said of the Big Macs. "Of course we ate the work horses last."

"Last after what?" I asked after I stopped laughing.

The sixty-year age difference didn't bother us a bit. The man could make me laugh. I liked his company, actually growing to prefer it to Daniel's although the sex with Daniel was still good, but I was spending a lot of time with Rudolf too.

And then, Rudolf made what Idio referred to as the Great Transition. He passed away in his sleep one night when Daniel and I were at a benefit dinner for his favorite charity, SUCS, the Survivers of Unhealthy Childhood Society.

He took the call on his ever-present designer cell phone, which he paid a service to call him periodically to enhance his appearance of importance, and fainted into the tureen of Chicken Comfort Soup they always served.

I wiped the bits of Chicken Comfort off his face and drove him home to his tastefully furnished apartment, mostly paid for by Rudolf where he threw himself theatrically yet quite carefully onto the gold colored, silk covered couch to hold his handsome head in his hands and wail, the red limousine and champagne celebration apparently forgotten.

I escaped to my own more Spartan apartment where I could cry in private for a gentle old man who had been my friend.

The next day I dragged my puffy-eyed, hollow-cheeked, sad, drooping body down to the yoga class where Idio counseled me to wear a red, preferably flamenco style dress and celebrate Rudolf's release.

It's all part of the ineffable beauty of the world," he said. "And it can only bring you closer to his grieving son."

"His grieving son is riffling through his father's possessions as we speak and there is no sex—I mean no thing in the world that can bring me closer to him," I cried.

I bought a sedate black dress and went with Daniel to the funeral parlor/chapel where I cried in the curtained off family mourning room as the fake preacher rattled off Rudolf's life's statistics and accomplishments and Daniel pretended to care.

The festivities, which moved to the cemetery, were a surrealistic blur of chubby, drunken relatives spitting mouthfuls of Gutzrotsk into the open grave on top of the floral arrangements, a family custom from the Old Country, Daniel explained. I took a mouthful of the vile semi-liquid but couldn't bring myself to spit on Rudolf's grave, so I swallowed the foul oily stuff and gagged as I cried all the way back to Rudolf's house where we ate and hugged and cried some more. Mostly the relatives ate and drank more of the Gutzrotsk.

Daniel decided we should leave early and hitch a ride in the mortuary limousine since the limo driver was the only sober adult in sight. We had to go back to the funeral home/chapel where we had left my car.

The limo driver, in addition to being sober, was a young, quite beautiful girl who looked really hot in the sedate, tailored grey pants suit and jaunty cap provided by the mortuary limo service.

Daniel, who had quaffed several shots of the traditional Gutzrotsk was, I realized, quite drunk; so drunk in fact that he was shamelessly leaning on the limo driver, his fine head nestled between her large breasts.

He had plopped himself down in the front seat beside her, leaving me alone in the back.

As I listened to his monologue, paying attention to the flow of my life, living in the Eternal Now, as Idio had instructed, I slowly realized it was a rerun. I had heard and seen it all before, the same smiles, the same longing look in his eyes, the same techniques Daniel had used on me.

It was the same line of crap that I had fallen for.

Good God! He was actually hitting on the hearse driver at his father's funeral! With me, his girlfriend in the back seat.

I reached for a tissue in the tasteful little red box on the seat beside me. Red box? Yes, red! The upholstery was red too, a muted, dark almost maroon red, but red nonetheless! I hit the electric window button and put my head out to be sure of the color of the outside of the limo and yes, it too was red, definitely red.

By then, Daniel had his beautifully manicured hand on the back of the blonde's neck and I made a decision, flow of life be damned. I also could divert and direct that flow. I was a veritable Hoover Dam of a diverter!

"Pull over to that drive-in liquor store window, Ms. Driver," I ordered. "Now."

She shoved Daniel's head off her ample chest and hastily did as I had asked. I bought a corkscrew and a bottle of the cheapest champagne in stock which I ordered in those very words, popped the cork which bounced off the windshield, whizzed by Daniel's head, ruffling his immaculately coiffed hair and ricocheted back by my ear to land somewhere in the rear of that big, ugly damn red limousine.

I took a big drink of the bubbly stuff, noting that the brand name was Quik Phix, told that blonde slut to pull over and crawled out of the limo, shaky but determined.

I handed Daniel the rest of the Quik Fix and walked away, not remembering or caring that it was still miles to my car.

"Your dream came true!" I shouted at Daniel as the red hearse/limousine pulled away. "You're free at last!"

"And so am I," I mumbled as I walked unsteadily off into the first evening of my Danieless life.

So Idio was right. I had documented proof now. You get what you want even if it sucks, even if you're a facetious, womanizing, cowardly, caricature of a man whose loving, kind 89 year old father has to die to get it for you.

But there is that cause/effect clause in the Agreement, you get what you give too, so somewhere, sometime, Daniel, there's an ungrateful, spoiled kid in a red limousine waiting for you too. Oh, the ineffable beauty and order of the world.

Idio says the doctrine of reincarnation is correct also. If it is and I hope so, Rudolf, let's synchronize our watches a little closer than sixty years next time and I'll meet you at the nearest McDonald's wearing my red flamenco dress. You don't have to bring any Gutzrotsk.

THE HUNDRED DOLLAR TIP

Their love affair began in the spring of '98 in the midst of the millennium madness just before the turn of the century.

It was a crazy time when tattooed giants who were paid unbelievable sums of money to compete in sporting events roamed the land, a time when the leaders of the free and also the not so free world were being impeached and recalled for such crimes as blow jobs and bad hair days, and this all made a bizarre sort of sense as the lines between entertainment, religion and politics had blurred; politics and religion had become show biz, presidential candidates were doing standup comedy on late night TV, evangelists with bad face lifts and big hair were singing rock songs about Jesus on gilt covered sets in front of TV cameras, and show business stars were the new royalty who also ran for office or espoused and supported political causes to a worldwide audience who worshipped at the altar of the Great God Media. The Media is indeed the message.

She would always speak of being on the rebound when she met him, but that was not technically accurate. It was really more of a dribble than a rebound because there were those three ex-lovers, all of whom fit a pattern as the psychologist the company sent her to pointed out.

"None of those guys were ready to settle down and raise a family," Dr. Samson said. "The musician was traveling with his band which even you called his mistress, the sculptor didn't even like kids and the race car driver was---"

"Suicidal and nuts," Sarah finished.

The lovers met in that psychologist's waiting room; he, oddly concave and faintly European with the lank hair of English royalty or a dying poet or both, and she, shy, beautiful and feeling as if she were at a crossroads in her life, not knowing which way to go.

She could imagine him writing poetry such as the heir to the throne had done, extolling the virtues of his royal mistress, longing to be a tampon so he could spend more quality time in that warm, wet, secure place in which he felt loved. Princehood must be lonely and hard.

It was only later that she could also imagine him capable of Druidicide or killing an innocent carob tree because it dropped leaves and seed pods he didn't want to rake up, not to mention its springtime emanations of a sweet, cloying odor that reminded him of hot, sweaty, sex soaked sheets in a shabby Nogales brothel.

Oh, she had been aware from the very beginning that he had problems, or life issues as their industrial psychologist preferred to call it. After all, they had met in Dr. Samson's waiting room.

She was thirty-four that spring, still slim, still lovely, still single. Her name was Sarah, and unlike that Biblical Sarah who gave birth at a hundred and ninety or thereabouts, this Sarah was disturbed by the imminent threat of the demise of her biological clock.

She had been having a recurring dream in which she was standing in a deep, dark, forbidding forest watching that clock through a pair of cheap throwaway 3D glasses.

It was a weird little clock made of slabs of crumbling gingerbread decorated with gooey, melted frosting, a cuckoo clock with a goofy little bird that looked like Daffy Duck who popped out on no particular time schedule to belch and sputter cuckoo, cuckoo at her.

She had been sent to the industrial psychologist by the company she worked for, an import export company that specialized in handwoven textiles. She was the international buyer for the Phoenix based company and she loved weaving and textiles in all their varied forms and splendor.

She loved the travel to seek out the silks and woolens, cottons and linens, the beautiful handmade blankets, shawls, garments, rugs and tapestries. She loved weaving and she loved learning of the various techniques and tools and she loved the weavers.

What she didn't love and what had landed her in Dr. Samson's office was a dislike for the rigid corporate world she had to return to in Phoenix. She was having an increasingly harder time accepting that world graciously. She had come to believe that the Japanese were right, middle management was unproductive and obsolete. It had been middle management who had sent her to Dr. Samson.

"Calling your CFO a pompous, boring, self-centered jackass isn't exactly conducive to a harmonious, good working condition," Dr. Samson said mildly as he scanned her file.

Sarah glared at him. "He referred to a handmade rug from Iran with more knots per square inch than his IQ as Product," she spat indignantly. "He called a Two Grey Hills Navajo rug with a hundred and twenty weft threads per inch that took a weaver a year and a half to finish, he called it a curio while complaining about the cost. He's a Philistine! All of those corporate people are Philistines. Some of them don't even know what the company PRODUCT is. They have tunnel vision, can only see their own little area of the freaking spreadsheets.

"I meet people from all over the world who work and produce, who dedicate their lives to their work while these people work on ways not to work."

Dr. Samson leaned back in his chair. She was right, he realized; most of the work force of America, who were his clients and employers, didn't know or care about their work except for the paycheck and the real or imagined prestige afforded by their increasingly more euphemistic job titles.

Dr. Samson, who had been a carpenter before he got a degree in psychology and who sometimes longed to return to carpentry, wore casual clothes to work, usually shorts and T-shirts even in Phoenix's mild winters.

The T-shirts had things printed on them like:
Wherever You Go, There You Are
Make the Payments and You Can Keep the Stuff
Your True Goal is Happiness
I Forgot the Question, But the Answer is Love

Joyce Keveren

E=MC Squared

Everything's Gonna Be Allright This Morning—Muddy Waters

The Rollin' Stones Gathered a LOT of Moss Santana Hears the Angels Sing and other things he thought his patients might like.

Sarah liked the one with a trade ad for Litenup, an antidepressant with some before and after pictures. Eeyore was before and Winnie the Pooh was After.

His sun-streaked light brown hair was long, almost to the middle of his back and his skin matched his hair, being only a shade or two lighter. His eyes were a startling clear green with flecks of gold, and were often filled with laughter, Sarah had noted. Not condescending amusement for the foibles of his patients, just real laughter.

He was about six feet tall, lean, but muscular and strong looking. The muscles were even and smooth, distributed well around his body, not the lumpy, distorted, vein-riddled out of proportion muscles achieved by working out. They looked as if he had done real work that needed done to get them, not lifting weights that didn't need lifting or running nowhere on a treadmill.

Sarah had already asked him if, like Samson, his strength came from his hair and did he avoid women with scissors.

He had grinned and said, yes, he never dated beauticians and returned to her problems, once more reading from her file.

"We are referring Sarah because she is unusually combative and uncooperative, disrespectful and recalcitrant, creating a hostile work environment," he read.

"Recalcitrant? Hostile? I guess so. Not only do those co-workers of mine not know a Bhutan blanket from a Columbian ruana, they don't CARE. Even though those blankets and ruanas, not to mention the weavers who make them, pay their salaries while they produce nothing. Some of them don't even understand their own jobs. They know they have to enter data into their computers but they don't know or care WHY. I couldn't work that way. I have to know what I'm doing and why I'm doing it. Even if I'm wrong, I have to know."

Dr. Samson agreed while questioning if he really knew what it was he was trying to do here as an industrial psychologist. Pound round pegs into square holes? As a carpenter, he wouldn't have to do that, he wouldn't even think of it. As a carpenter he could do something he actually knew he could do. Oh, yes, he knew she was right and the Philistines she spoke of had hired him to 'fix' her. What if she didn't need 'fixing' and it was the aforementioned Philistines who needed 'fixing'?

He cleared his throat and referred to her case file again. Usually he did not reveal the contents of a client's file so directly to the client, but something about this one intrigued him and made him reckless. But, to be fair to me, he thought, she literally demanded to know what they said to land her here in my office. Maybe I'm just trying to entertain myself by stirring her up was an uncomfortable thought that occurred to him. He plunged ahead anyway. "However," he said, "you can't refer to them, your co-workers in person as 'you blind, pompous, self-serving egotistical useless assholes," he read, then looked up at her, "accurate though it might be."

In their subsequent sessions which Sarah was beginning to enjoy, they discussed things not related to work, things like her Daffy Duck biological cuckoo clock dream and her desire for children.

"I know there are 7 billion people on this planet, a regular infestation and I know maybe it's just a selfish wish to perpetuate me. I know it may be nothing more than a biological imperative that should have been eliminated by evolution some time back like tails, but I still want babies and a live-in father and husband to help raise them."

"You don't have to apologize for that," Samson said. "That's normal."

"And I don't want to be normal either," Sarah said adamantly. "I got sent here in the first place by those 'normal' people willing to spend their lives in little cubicles like rats doing work that's debatable whether it even needs done."

And who was he to determine who's normal and who isn't. Just because he's got a degree in psychology or whatever it is.

The more she hung around his office building, the harder it became to distinguish between doctors and patients. And wasn't he the one with the Samson complex, so attached to his damn hair he had a blow dryer in his bathroom at work and an irrational fear of women with scissors?

Joyce Keveren

On the day she confessed her longing for a soul mate, lover, father of her children type man instead of the wandering types she had been dating, Dr. Samson escorted her out to the waiting room where his next client waited.

"This is Michael, Sarah," he said.

Michael stood up to take her hand in his.

It had seemed like destiny to Sarah. He looked like a movie star/politician, his dark hair perfectly cut and styled, no Delilah phobia there, his three hundred-dollar Italian shoes polished to a fare-thee-well, his suit perfectly fitted to his somewhat odd frame and posture.

Dr. Samson later told her in a self-confessed and blatant violation of the sacred doctor-patient code of confidentiality that Michael too wanted to settle down and raise a family.

Of little sunken-chested Michael clones wearing immaculately tailored three piece suits and Italian loafers with tassels he thought but kept to himself in a moment of superb self-control because he realized that Sarah, the beautiful Sarah who could summon such passion for handwoven rugs, my God, what would she be like if she loved someone with that much passion? Or hated someone that much was the next thought that hit his head. It didn't matter because she was already falling for Michael.

Michael had been referred to him by his colleagues in the large, successful law firm in which he had already become a junior partner. The senior partners had referred him, reluctantly they said, because he was a bit too aggressive in soliciting clients. Good God, he's a lawyer in an ambulance chasing firm of piranhas and he's too aggressive? He must be a regular Great White Shark Samson thought.

He wanted to warn Sarah, but he knew it was too late. She was already gone, lost in a Cinderella haze of infatuation.

She did, however, mention to Dr. Samson that Michael was obsessed with the shine of his expensive shoes.

It was a full year before she realized that with his feet placed just so, at exactly the right distance and angle, those shoes would act as mirrors reflecting what was up the skirt of any woman he stood near.

She learned that accidentally as she watched him fidget as they stood in line to get into Banditi's, the most exclusive and overpriced pasta place in the city. She glanced down where he was absorbed in looking at his shoes and beheld the crotch of the young woman in front of him.

Did Dr. Samson know about this? Did it explain Michael's strange, hunched over posture which both she and Dr. Samson had attributed to an off-center hunchbacked curling of the body in an attempt to protect himself or return to the womb perhaps?

"Only if it's his own womb he's returning to," Dr. Samson muttered to himself. "His first and only love."

But that night in front of Banditi's with a city full of orange blossoms perfuming the air and a year of plans and discussions about raising a family behind them, Sarah was still besotted with him so she gave him the benefit of the doubt. Maybe he was only looking at the cracks in the pavement or the reflections of the street lights in that puddle of oily water. Maybe she was the goofy one looking up at the pantyhosed butt of a young stranger.

He didn't do it all the time, after all, mostly in crowds and he did take her to the most expensive restaurants in town where pasta sold for $100 a pound. He also took her to the symphony and the opera, to the theatres and concerts, to the galleries and the art shows where she could dress up in sequins and velvet or spandex and denim or whatever else she wanted. And he was professionally and financially successful and most important, he wanted to settle down and raise a family. With her.

They had even discussed and worked out a plan that would enable Sarah to continue to go on her much-loved buying trips; Michael could take a leave of absence from his work for a week or two at a time to watch the hypothetical children.

It all seemed so perfect, but there was one little thing that nagged at her even worse than the shiny shoes or the Daffy Duck cuckoo clock.

It was this: The sex was pretty good, mostly because she had fallen in love, but it was also a bit rapid fire and pedestrian, yet desperate and—the only other word she could come up with—furtive. Not like lovers with a hailstorm of bullets ricocheting willy-nilly around them in some gutted war zone or guilty adulterers evading an outraged, armed spouse, but more like someone afraid of the position some invented Deity might be taking on their union or worse, a fear of the act itself coupled with an even greater fear of female sexuality and its power to entrap.

"Not uncommon in men," Dr. Samson told her when she expressed her thoughts to him. "Since the dawn of time, since the first woman gave birth to the first child, and later too, when men first looked down in wonder at their one-eyed alternate brain and realized it had contributed to reproduction, and along with that, their realization of the ominous implications of lifetime responsibility, which led to the male dominate socio-religious quagmire of the last 10,000 years or more and especially with the recent discovery of the female orgasm, men have been terrified of female sexuality."

"You too, Dr. S? Or only if the women are packing shears?"

Dr. Samson was not eager to investigate Michael's phobias, and if he did, he realized that he would need an industrial shrink himself because it would only be for the sole purpose of exposing Michael in all his tarnished horror to Sarah because he, Samson, was falling in love with her himself.

And why not? She was beautiful, passionate and smart, with skin like ripened peaches, long shapely legs and eyelashes long enough to wrap around his little finger and those dark eyes full of fire and laughter.

No, he would have to let her discover for herself yet another mistake in her choice of men.

That is, if she didn't wind up pregnant when it might be too late.

But Michael did confide in him. At Sarah's urging, he told Dr. Samson of the source of his fear and revulsion.

He told him of the recurring vision of that sweaty, drunken whore in Nogales that his Uncle Jake, that drunken old reprobate had rented for him the summer he was sixteen.

"I can still hear her derisive laughter, still smell the acrid odor in that sleazy room, still see the reflection of the flashing neon sign outside the grimy window."

"What was it?" Samson asked.

"What was what?" Michael demanded.

"The sign. What did it say?"

Michael's face registered annoyance. "What's that got to do with anything?" he asked.

Dr. Samson shrugged.

"The sign said Pedro's Tamales, muy caliente. To this day I can't eat a tamale. Not even at Christmas in Phoenix where it's a tradition."

"You could starve here if you don't eat tamales," Dr. Samson said. Michael glared at him.

"Sorry," Samson said. "Please go on."

"It was raining and I wanted to cry but that degenerate alcoholic uncle of mine was clapping me on the back and whinnying like a goddamn work horse as we walked through the rain back to his car."

Dr. Samson smothered an urge to tell this whining, self-pitying, over fastidious, self-loving misogynistic, elitist butthead to check himself into the nearest monastery for a lifetime commitment where he need never come into contact with a woman again. Especially Sarah.

Or better yet, join a cult that made eunuchs of its male devotees to keep them pure before the mothership picked them up for their trip to God's Place.

Or just drive your goddamn Porsche off a cliff, kill yourself, you fatuous freak—

He finally derailed that thought train and took refuge in a question. "What do you think you could do to resolve this problem?"

"That's what my law firm is paying you for," Michael said in a voice loaded with scorn.

Dr. Samson tried to compose his thoughts. If I retired as a psychologist and went back to being a finish carpenter, I could actually tell this guy what I think of him. I love carpentry, but I'm beginning to love Sarah too, so that option is out.

He sighed and took refuge in the platitude section of Psychology 101 in an effort to placate the overdressed, prissy freak the woman of his dreams had fallen for, and get him out of his office.

He suggested role playing, meditation, prayer, some strenuous physical activity, a change of diet, a vacation, anything that would break the daily established pattern of living and thinking.

Maybe those hair transplants that looked like neat rows of an Iowa cornfield had sent roots down into his brain and would eventually kill him, Dr. Samson thought. Thank God he couldn't get his license revoked for his thoughts even though his hapless patients could be medicated and committed for the voices in their heads.

Life isn't fair. It sure as hell isn't when that prick has Sarah and I don't.

"The best way to rid yourself of this negative memory is to establish a strong, loving relationship with a caring woman who loves you," he said, the words sticking in his throat.

"Yeah, sure," Michael said. "I've done that."

A vision of Sarah came into Dr. Samson's mind, Sarah in that gauzy white handwoven dress with the red flowers on it, her dark hair loose around her shoulders, her long legs and slender feet bare.

"I need something else," Michael was saying. "Now."

"What sometimes works is a visit to the location of the trauma, a reenactment of sorts. Perhaps you should speak frankly to your uncle also."

"That fool drank himself to death years ago," Michael stated. "But a visit to the place, a re-run, now that might help."

"Do only what feels comfortable to you," Dr. Samson advised, adding in his head, you misogynistic son of a bitch as a self-satisfied Michael left his office, his Italian shoes gleaming under the lights.

Michael invited Sarah on his planned trip to Nogales, the trip that led to the Druidicide that became the spur to Sarah's awakening.

He drove the cream-colored Porsche south out of Phoenix on a day of glorious sunshine and gentle breezes through the Sonoran Desert in all its spring glory of red blooming ocotillo, red and yellow prickly pear, the delicate yellow blossoms of the palo verde lighting up the arroyos. Even the saguaro with their little crown of white flowers were in bloom.

By midafternoon they were in Nogales, Arizona where Michael found an all-night gas station willing to let him park the Porsche so he didn't have to drive it across the border.

They walked across the border after a late lunch hand in hand to a waiting line of taxis of various models in equally varied states of decay or regeneration.

Sarah chose a '67 Dodge Charger with patches of white scattered around its body where careful body work had removed the scars and dents of the years. All it lacked was a new paint job. It looked like a spirited paint horse ready to go.

The driver, whose hand lettered name tag said Miguel Cervantes, waved at them and smiled. He was a small, wiry man of about 35 with dark eyes and curly dark hair cut short and a fine, curved nose that looked to Sarah like it belonged on a Mayan carving.

"She runs good," he said in English as he patted the Charger and gave Sarah an appreciative smile.

Michael asked to be taken to a place with a sign that said Pedro's Hot Tamales and the Charger leaped forward.

Miguel, keeping one strong brown hand on the wheel, turned to look at them, asking a long question in Spanish.

Sarah realized he had naturally assumed they were hungry and wanted to know what restaurant they wanted to go to and where it was.

She told Michael who said, "Tell him to go to all of them. I'm looking for that sign. I think it was on the west side of the city."

Sarah tried in her halting, inadequate Spanish to relay the message to Miguel who nodded.

He took them to every restaurant, café and sidewalk food stand on the west side, but Michael didn't recognize anything.

Miguel glanced back at Sarah with a puzzled expression on his lively face.

"Tell him you want a whorehouse, Michael," Sarah said.

"For God's sake, Sarah," Michael exploded. "How crude."

"Oh, si, senorita," Miguel said with a big grin.

"I'm crude? You're the one on a mission to a whore house," Sarah said as her eyes met Miguel's in the rear-view mirror where a rosary dangled. She wondered how much English Miguel understood.

God only knows what Miguel thought.

Miguel whipped a U-turn in the dirt of the side road they were on, one as good as that ex-lover, the race car driver could do and the pinto Charger leaped forward again.

In less than fifteen minutes, Miguel spotted the building he remembered from almost fifteen years earlier. It was still there, still dilapidated and still in business.

Miguel, obviously bewildered and intrigued by two goofy, yet rich looking Norteamericanos, the young lady gorgeous in her red flowered dress, would not hear of leaving Sarah alone while the crazed senor went in search of a whore.

Perhaps too, there would be a good tip which he could use. There was yet another baby on the way at home.

He accompanied Sarah to the bar where they seated themselves at a little wrought iron table while Michael was directed toward the back down a long dark hallway with many doors opening off it on both sides.

Sarah ordered margaritas for herself and Miguel from the bartender as a mariachi band began to play.

"La musica es muy bueno aqui," Miguel said.

She nodded and sipped her drink. It was good too. "I love mariachis," she told Miguel. "And margaritas."

Thirty minutes passed in which they conversed in a mixture of English, Spanish and sign language and listened to the band.

At first she glanced nervously back down that long hall for Michael occasionally, but by the time they were on their second margarita, she stopped looking except to note that couples would now and then wander away down the hall to disappear through one of the doorways. She relaxed and enjoyed the music.

"Me llamo Miguel Cervantes," Miguel said formally as he led her to the worn dance floor where several couples were already dancing. Evidently for him, dancing required a formal introduction.

"I'm Sarah," she told him.

In a very short while, she found herself easily following Miguel's fluid salsa movements, enjoying herself very much.

"It's all in the hips," he instructed as he gestured and demonstrated.

They danced until the Mariachi band took a break and the bartender came by their table to bring one more margarita.

Sarah checked her money. She had enough left for one more drink and tips. Good thing the margaritas were not too strong or I'd be under the table she thought with a giggle. But I'm okay, I feel safe with Miguel. How odd. I don't feel safe with Michael a lot of the time, a vague feeling of discontent mixed with a mild fear and I feel safe with this perfect stranger. But the perfect stranger was treating her with respect. Well, there was her emergency fund, the hundred-dollar bill she had tucked behind her driver's license, but margaritas in a Nogales brothel weren't exactly on her list of emergencies. Not yet anyway.

Miguel spoke to the bartender in Spanish, a rapid-fire string of words in which Sarah caught please, guitar and flamenco.

"He will play for us now," Miguel told her.

"Music from the angels."

With a guilty start, Sarah looked around for Michael. She had forgotten about him again in the enjoyment of the dancing. Where was he?

The bartender pulled off his apron, grabbed a guitar from a case behind the bar and sat on a stool Miguel pulled out for him.

He began to play in flamenco style, his long fingers touching the strings so quickly Sarah's eyes could barely follow the movement.

His hands were beautiful, his fingers long and strong, and they touched the strings with such gentle, loving sureness that Sarah was entranced. And the music that came from that guitar, was, as Miguel had said, heavenly and soaring, rising and falling, floating through the room and embracing everyone.

He played the joy of life and he played the sorrow of life and they were one and the same thing, just pure notes interwoven into one beautiful melody. The guitar seemed to be saying that if everything else is gone and there's only the music left, then that is enough. That is enough to create a whole new world.

The people in the bar ceased their chattering, glasses were no longer being rattled as the young man played, weaving his magic spell. Once again, Sarah forgot all about Michael.

When the last note faded away and the young man put the guitar away to once again don his bartender's apron, the people waited a moment for the spell to be broken and slowly began to applaud.

Sarah gave the rest of her money, except for the emergency fund, to the bartender/flamenco guitarist as a tip. "You need one of those flamenco hats," she whispered to him.

The mariachi band assembled again and soon the dance floor was crowded and the noise began again.

It became so noisy they didn't hear the sirens until the front doors opened and several Federales burst into the smoke-filled room.

Two of them carried rifles as well as the pistols on their hips. Their brown uniforms were immaculate and well fitted.

Sarah, seated at the table with Miguel, saw Michael emerge headfirst from the hallway to the back rooms, his shirt tail flapping, his jacket ripped and blood streaming from a wound on his head.

He lay sprawled on the floor, moaning, with blood leaking from the cut on his head.

Miguel, sensing a large reward, managed to spirit Michael quickly away, out a back door, past the shrieking woman who had hit Michael, and safely into the Charger before the Federales arrested him and locked him up, maybe forever as he put it.

Sarah had done as Miguel had ordered, and walked calmly out the front door to meet them in the parking lot at the side of the building.

They sped into the night and back to the border crossing where Miguel told officials on both sides whatever they needed to hear to get his taxi through.

As they pulled up at the garage where they had left the Porsche, Michael was still gingerly probing his wounds.

He cursed and wiped blood off with his immaculate, monogrammed Irish linen handkerchief. "That bitch hit me with a full bottle of beer!" he yelped. "I'll sue her! I'll sue her whole goddamn organization!"

"You're gonna sue a whorehouse, Michael?" Sarah asked.

"You've got a lawyer?" Miguel asked.

"I AM a lawyer!" Michael screamed. "I'll sue the Mexican government! I'll sue the Federales!"

Miguel looked at Sarah and shrugged, his fine lips curving into a small smile. His glance took in the Porsche. "The lawyers in Mexico aren't doing so well. They're all starving. There is no problem in Nogales that can't be solved over a quart of Tecate."

Tecate was, in fact, the brand of beer the enraged whore had hit Michael with.

Miguel briefly and quickly explained to Sarah what he had heard from the whore lady.

"The whore lady hit him with a full bottle of Tecate and then called the Federales because he," he gestured toward Michael who was still cursing and mumbling, "because he insult her job, her life, her sex, her establishment and her integrity. I heard her yell it all to the Federales before we left. And she thought he was muy loco too."

Michael was still wiping blood off his head. He cursed all women, all whores, all whorehouses, his deceased uncle, the government of Mexico and Dr. Samson, but most of all Dr. Samson.

Sarah, full of tequila and appreciation for the lovely, lively dancing and the mariachi band, but mostly for the flamenco guitarist/bartender, laughed until she cried which only made Michael more angry.

"Get in the car!" he yelled at her.

"Pay Miguel," she said, her voice leaving no room for dissent.

"How much?" he asked Miguel in a savage tone as he got his wallet out.

Miguel named a figure that was quite reasonable, adding that he hadn't charged for the time he waited for Michael at the whorehouse because dancing with the lovely senorita was so very nice.

Michael paid him the fee and turned to get in the Porsche.

"Aren't you going to give him a tip, Michael?" Sarah asked in an enraged tone.

Michael turned to glare at her. "A tip? I almost get killed and he wants a tip?"

"He saved your ass, Michael! You'd be in the custody of the Federales if he hadn't snuck you out right by that enraged woman you insulted."

"I safed your ass," Miguel echoed.

Sarah had a sudden startled realization that Miguel's English had greatly improved. It was very good in fact.

Michael got in the Porsche, slammed the door and started the engine.

Sarah dug in her purse and handed Miguel the hundred-dollar bill, all she had left. This was a bonafide emergency, her list be damned, and too, she distinctly heard the sounds of that otherworldly guitar in her head.

Joyce Keveren

Miguel took a look at the folded bill, grabbed her and hugged her tight, then kissed her long and hard. "Gracias," he said as he looked into her eyes. "I will not forget you. I will never forget you. My next baby, due any day now will be called Sarah. May the blessed Virgin of Guadalupe grant you long life, much happiness and many children."

Michael, his battered head poking out the window, gunned the motor, all 413 horses raring to go. "Get in," he yelled. "How much did you give him to get that kind of response and what was that crap about naming a baby?"

She got in the car with one last look at Miguel who waved at her. "A hundred bucks," she told Michael, her voice like frost on a bottle of Tecate.

"A hundred-dollar tip for a taxi driver who took us only twenty kilometers?"

She didn't answer and he drove like a maniac all the way home, risking arrest once more.

He dropped her off at her home with only a curt nod and sped away.

So she stayed away from him, refusing to answer his calls, avoiding places he might be such as Samson's office. She didn't even answer her door.

A month went by. She dreamed Daffy Duck moved out of her cuckoo clock and flew south toward Nogales for the winter where he was building a two-story nest in what looked like the bell tower of a church.

Then she began to think she was pregnant and a home pregnancy test confirmed it.

She went to see Michael and discovered he had chopped down the lovely old carob tree in his back yard. It was gone, not even a stump remained. He had hired a tree service to remove it in a fit of anger, a rerun of his Nogales rage the day after he got home.

"It smelled like sex, like that whore's room," he said. "And it was filthy and messy."

To wantonly kill a tree in the water poor Sonoran Desert was a crime that Sarah could not condone and one she couldn't understand either.

"I'm pregnant, Michael," she said quietly, feeling sad about the tree and about many other things too.

"That's wonderful," he shouted. "We'll get married. We'll---"

"No," Sarah said. "We won't."

He wailed and yelled, cajoled and pleaded until he realized he must use his big guns.

He threatened to use the combined power of his entire law firm and take the baby from her the moment the cord was cut. He would have his child, he said, if she wouldn't marry him or live with him, he would take it from her. Legally.

She listened to this diatribe for only a moment longer as she looked at the empty space where the old carob tree had been, the tree whose only crime had been dropping leaves and pods and smelling like sex.

That tree was a lot like me, she thought as a flight mechanism took over her brain. She got up and ran for the side gate.

"I mean it, Sarah! You're crazy!"

She stopped and unlatched the gate, prepared to bolt for her car. And then she heard the song of the flamenco guitarist of Nogales playing in her head and the Idea came to her. "You don't want this baby, Michael. It's not yours."

"Not mine?"

"You asked why I would give a taxi driver who saved your ass a hundred-dollar tip, remember? Think about it." She paused and locked him right in the eye. "It's Miguel's baby." Miguel, Michael, it's all the same.

She watched his face change from rage to disbelief and back to rage, a crumpling effect like someone had wadded up a piece of aluminum foil. My God, she thought, he actually bought it. He's been a lawyer way too long now. He can't identify a lie to save his life.

Five months later, Dr. Samson, wearing a T-shirt that said, It's a wise father who knows his own child, was reading yet another referral for Sarah.

This one said: Arguing with a superior and disobeying a direct order not to go on buying trip to Guatemala. Called superior a sexist moron.

So she was mellowing a bit; there were no swearwords reported so far.

Just then Sarah waddled in, her six-month pregnancy revealed under a beautiful and delicate dress made from the finest hand-woven Guatemalan fabric available.

Samson laughed as he realized the reason the company had requested she not go to Guatemala.

"What's so funny?" she asked.

"So you and that—Michael got married?" he asked as he shuffled some papers around on his desk.

"No. We did not."

"Why not?"

"I refuse to marry a tree killing jerkoff who doesn't like the smell of sex and carob trees. And when I told him it's not his baby, he didn't want to marry me anymore." She glanced at the case file in his hand. "And I could damn well buy textiles six months pregnant. I did it. Check out this fabric."

She quickly told him most of the story, adding her misgivings about raising a child alone and depriving a child of its father as she read the message on his shirt. He sure loved those refutations of old saws.

"But you said Miguel had a wife and many children. You can't do a thing about it without depriving those children of a father. So it's a question of degree here, don't you think?"

Geez, Sarah thought. Everybody believes that bullshit story. So why can't I just start believing it too? Maybe that spell of the flamenco guitar had done it or the intervention of the Virgin of Guadalupe as Miguel had said. Where do babies really come from anyway?

"I will not raise a child with Michael," she said fiercely. "If he wants a kid he should just get himself cloned unless he can get one to spring full grown from his forehead. He'd be a bad influence on a kid. How would you like to have him raise your kid?" she asked Samson defiantly.

Samson heartily agreed with her, but he only nodded his professional I see nod and stayed silent.

"So I guess it's just me and little Miguel here and no more trips for now," Sarah said as she pushed herself up out of the chair.

"Would you and little Miguel like to go out for dinner and a movie?" Dr. Samson asked, his voice cracking. "With me?"

She looked at him, read his T-shirt one more time and said, "Yes. Yes, I would. We'd like that."

THE LETTER

Ada was old, not just getting old as her sister in Oregon had been saying for twenty years, but undeniably, already there, old.

She had turned 86 on her last birthday. And it was all right with her. Most of the time.

Her son Paul had been running the little ranch her late husband had left her. Paul was a good manager and a good son. He had nearly finished renovating the old bunkhouse for her to move into which would give his family more room and more privacy in the old ranch house.

He had done all the wiring and plumbing himself and he had insulated it well and installed an old folks tub and shower, new kitchen cabinets and beautiful new flooring she had chosen herself at the Rancher's Lumber Company over in Muddy Flat, the little town of 2500 people where they did their shopping. The propane floor heater was ready to go when winter hit too.

She was happy about her short move to the pretty new home and grateful to Paul for doing all that hard work. She especially loved those new kitchen cabinets he had hung. She had already put her old set of dishes with the wild rose pattern away in them and the new propane cook stove worked well.

She bought a new bed and a living room couch and recliner at Anderson's in Muddy Flat. The couch and chair were in a lovely color the salesman called mauve, but she called it dusty rose. She made curtains for all four of the rooms and bought some warm wool rugs for the floors to put over the high-tech fake wood flooring. It got cold in the winters here on the high northern plains. Her clothes were all arranged in the closet and dressers. All she needed to do now was finish going through all that little bit of stuff left stored in the closet in her old ranch house bedroom. She had already thrown out a lot of old stuff that nobody needed or wanted and she was ready to finish the job. There were only the top shelves in the bedroom closet that needed cleaned out. It's always good, she had told her sister who was a writer, to clean house when starting a new chapter in your life.

Especially when some of those chapters had not been happy or good, but miserable and full of discontent and despair. That's the kind of thing I want to throw out, she thought as she wound her long grey hair into a messy knot on top of her head. She put on an old shirt and pair of pants and headed to the back room.

The closet was already nearly cleaned out. This room would become Paul's twin girls' room when the new baby arrived in a few months. He had moved her two old dressers into the new house and she had given the old brass bed to Jennie, Paul's wife. There was nothing left but that top shelf in the closet she hadn't looked at since her husband died some ten years before.

She was alone in the house, but she got out the stepladder and set it up so she could reach to the back, not heeding Paul's warning about climbing on things at her age. Paul was out tending to the sheep and Jennie and the girls were visiting Jennie's mother in Spearfish across the state line in South Dakota this week.

She would be careful. And waiting would only insure that she was older, maybe even more rickety, so she took her shoes off and climbed up. She held on to the edge of the shelf to steady herself and reached back.

The first thing her fingers touched was an umbrella her sister had sent her from Oregon where everybody had an umbrella on the southern coast where it rained a hundred inches a year. Here in southeast Montana on the Great Plains where ten inches a year was a good year, nobody had an umbrella. Little kids splashed in puddles and Ada had been known to dance in the rain with her face held up to feel the drops and the ranchers and farmers all rejoiced each in their own way.

She kept the umbrella because it had Van Gogh's sunflowers on it which her sister knew was one of her favorite paintings. She decided to clean it up and hang it somewhere in her room, maybe upside down from the ceiling so the sunflowers would show. She dropped it carefully to the floor.

Then she found the old hat box from a store in Billings that had been her mother's. She got carefully down off the stool and opened the box, inspected the two ridiculous old hats with the drooping feathers and old-fashioned veils than had belonged to her mother. She dusted them carefully and put them back in the box and left it for the twins to play with.

She climbed back up on the step stool and found one more object at the back of the top shelf. It was a small cedar chest with a picture of Mount Rushmore on it that had belonged to her mother-in-law, dead now for forty years. That's probably why I never touched it or looked at it she thought to herself, remembering all the lectures and criticism and downright condemnation and cruelty the old woman had lavished on her. She was amazed that her fear of the ornery old woman was still there inside her.

"Well, she's gone and I need to clean this place up," she said to herself as she opened the box. It was filled with old newspaper clippings, some so old they were yellowed and crumbling.

She picked up the top one. It was a report of the birth of the old woman's first child, Isaac, who had been Ada's husband, cut from the Muddy Flat Monday Bugle that everyone laughed about because it often came out on any day but Monday. There were birth announcements for Abe, Isaac's younger brother and their sister Cora, death notices of people Ada had not known, but the names were familiar to her, local ranchers and farmers.

There were a few ribbons from local 4-H livestock shows and one Isaac had won in a horse show and three old photos, one for each of her children.

And resting on the very bottom of the little box was a folded piece of lined notebook paper. She went out to the living room to sit down to read it. She unfolded it and read it very quickly, then read it again.

Joyce Keveren

It was a love letter from forty years ago to someone named Tim. There was a date, but no signature at the end, but that was surely her late husband Isaac's handwriting. He was not a good speller or writer, and those mistakes, aboud for about, thinking aboud you, and those cramped small letters were his style too. It may not have been signed, but that was Isaac's handwriting all right.

No, it couldn't be. It's a love letter, Isaac had never loved anybody. Except Amanda, their daughter, if that brand of spoiling could be called love. If anyone fit that word spoiled, it was that child, who had turned into that middle-aged matron who was still spoiled. Everyone around her still lived with the bitter results of that love.

Ada tucked the letter carefully into the pocket of her sweater, climbed up once again to clean the dust off the shelf, got down and dusted the little cedar box and put a note on it for Paul, saying the old hats are for the girls to play with and this box belonged to your grandmother.

She went to her new home and carefully laid the letter on top of her dresser where she had put the yellow doily with the purple pansies on it she had crocheted, then reconsidered and laid it on the top of the larger of the two dressers, the one that had been Isaac's. She decided she would hang the umbrella in her bedroom.

She took a bath in the new tub and ate some grapes and cheese, read the letter again, still wondering who Tim was. Then she remembered some things. There had been clues all along. She thought of Muddy Flat, that little cow town and rail head up here in the coal and oil and cattle country they were raised in, its climate of suspicion and intolerance and her late husband's frantic and aggressive pursuit of her, as if his very life depended on her marrying him. That ended in her pregnancy with Paul. After that, his indifference to her that gradually became rejection, took over. He was often gone from the ranch, mostly because of his blatant womanizing, leaving a couple of kids around here and there that he referred to as catch colts when not denying their very existence. She thought of the constant anger and unhappiness and self-pity that manifested itself in outbursts of cruelty to her and their two kids, mostly Paul. For some reason Amanda was immune. Well, the indifference was welcome actually, anything that kept him away from her was good. And it had never been a love match, not even close, but their relationship would have earned a gold medal if hatred had been an Olympic event.

Living on a small farm and ranch with just a few head of cattle and a couple of cornfields, Isaac often tried to supplement their meager income with outside work, and he often hired members of the community to help him with the work.

One year, it was putting up hay for other ranchers and farmers with larger, more prosperous spreads. He hired two young men that summer to help him. She couldn't remember who those young men were, but maybe the sons of the German family over north of Muddy Flat with the wheat farm.

He borrowed money from his mother to buy the mower and hay baler and tractors and at the end of the summer, tired of this work, he sold all the equipment at a farm auction at a pretty good loss, didn't pay his mom back so there was a small profit for a lot of work.

That memory led to another, that whole summer he spent wandering around the sawmills of northern Wyoming, southern Montana, and eastern South Dakota, cornering the market in sawdust. There wasn't much of a market so it had been easy.

His brother Abe, who worked in the oil fields, somehow had an idea that sawdust would solve an oil drilling problem called lost circulation. Much to the delight of the sawmill owners, they bought tons of sawdust from Deadwood and Lead in South Dakota, Newcastle and Sundance in Wyoming and everywhere else they found any, stored it in an old warehouse that had been built to store the wool crop in the area they rented in Ekalaka, Montana, all ready to sell at a massive profit to all those rich oil drillers.

The two brothers spent one whole spring, summer and fall on the ill-fated project while their mother complained and blamed Ada and Ada and the two kids kept the farm going and she once again had to go back to work at the Old Time Country Kitchen over in Muddy Flat.

"Just you wait," Isaac would tell her and the kids and his increasingly disgruntled mother. "This time, me and Abe are gonna hit a lick and make some real money."

Then the warehouse burned down in a mighty blaze that lit up the night and gave the residents of Ekalaka something to laugh and talk about.

"That sawdust is damn sure flammable," Abe announced like he had just learned it.

Their mother, who had always favored Isaac, blamed the whole thing on Abe with some help from Ada who, she contended was just too demanding for what she called 'high falutin' stuff' no farm wife needs. Ada remembered that she had been relieved to have Abe to share the blame with this time.

Isaac always bragged about what a hard worker he was and after about twenty years of hearing that and adding up the losses of those ventures, and at the end of the sawdust adventure that took years to pay off, she dared to say to him one day when he was whining and yelling about how hard he worked and how little she did to help, she said, "Working hard is good, but maybe working smart would be better, do something that works," a brave statement that earned her a vicious slap that knocked her glasses off and left her with a black eye. He blamed her for breaking her glasses and refused to let her buy a new pair so she went without until she could afford a new pair from her wages at the café in Muddy Flat.

That memory pissed her off, so she stomped around her new house for a bit until she recalled another failed scheme, the bronc breaking plan which included buying twenty or thirty unbroken young horses from the sale barn over in Belle Fourche, building a round corral and paying some young men to help break the horses. The loss was considerable although the sale barn did pretty well on the operation.

This endeavor too had required a couple of young men to work it. The old round corral was still out there, the heavy posts rotting slowly. Paul didn't break horses, preferring to check on the livestock on his old Honda motorcycle.

When Paul took over the ranch, he gradually built up a registered herd of Columbia sheep that thrived on the southern Montana plains. That herd of sheep that his father was too stubborn and proud as a cattleman to run was still supporting the family very well, with two paydays every year instead of just one from the cattle. Paul had also upgraded the herd of Hereford cattle with registered polled bulls so the place was prosperous now.

Paul's wife was a school teacher, and unlike his father, he had not demanded she work while blabbering all over the country how his wife would never have to work. Ada was proud of Paul and his work was not only hard, but smart too.

She made herself a cup of tea, using the new teapot her sister had sent her as a house warming gift. It had sunflowers on it too. She sat down in the new dusty rose recliner and switched on the TV, then fell asleep for a bit, woke up remembering other things from so long ago, shut off the TV so she could think better. Who was Tim? Her train of thought took her to that old book of Ayn Rand's that she used to love with its question of Who is John Galt? Reading had always been her pastime, education and salvation.

She remembered how she had noted in the early years, Isaac's adoring, reverent tone of voice when speaking of a high school teacher he had, a man from back east who taught boys physical education. Isaac, who was usually very disrespectful of anything connected to formal education after he dropped out of school, would say this man's name as though it was sacred, as though he had been a lover, something she learned when she fell in love for the first time herself.

When she asked Isaac's brother Abe about this teacher, she remembered he had laughed and said, "Yeah, I remember that queer. We ran him out of town. Probably saved his sorry ass, before he got beaten to death."

There had been other things she noticed too, like the way he would sit with his legs crossed high up like a woman even though it wasn't comfortable for a man with a heavy barrel chest above his short, stocky legs, that, like his massive belly, kept getting fatter with the passing of the years. And the way he began to look more and more like his dead mother, that mean, meddlesome, masculine, bored old woman with the fat flapping upper arms and black mustache whose total aim in life seemed to be tormenting her daughter-in-law.

All those years, all that cruelty. Ada had dreamed of leaving him and never could, she had no education, no family support from that pack of crazed Baptists in northern Wyoming, the ones who believed that divorce brought eternal burning damnation in Hell. Those Welsh, Irish, Scotch, English, Dutch folks with all those stiff upper lips had taught her their brand of denial, raising it to an art form. They could successfully ignore and lie about anything that didn't fit into their narrow view of the world.

She had grown up with lies and pretense and learned it well, along with the submissive role of women.

She had once overheard the manager of the Country Kitchen tell another co-worker that 'Ada takes humility way too far'. And fear of the old woman and Isaac kept it alive. There was no Dr. Phil to tell her she had rights, no counselors or psychiatrists back then. Indeed, there were still no counselors in Muddy Flat. You were on your own, something those tough old pioneers and their descendants took great pride in. Not even Oprah could change them. Ada was trapped.

Until Isaac died and she was free. But now she was old. And still poor, but since she was in control of her own money, her small Social Security check, and didn't have to give everything to Isaac for his addictions and pastimes and money-losing schemes, it was enough.

The old resentments she was stirring up in her head made her feel guilty, but it was also bringing some more memories to the surface.

She remembered another one of Isaac's grandiose plans one year was to buy dairy calves in Wisconsin where he had been assured they were dirt cheap, haul them home to the ranch and bottle feed and care for them until they could be sold for beef. So many died during that hard winter, some of them dying by the old wood cookstove in the kitchen, smelling of the scours they died of.

With the pickup and stock trailer expenses to haul them on the long trips to Wisconsin, the veterinarian bills and the cost of the feed, those losses were monumental. That spring with dead black and white Holstein calves littering the back forty and Mama no longer eager to shell out money to her spoiled son, Ada had first taken her job waiting tables in Muddy Flat to make ends meet. That year, the kids were in fourth and sixth grade, still attending the country school near the ranch.

That failed enterprise had required the help of a couple young men too. One of them rode along to Wisconsin on all four trips to buy those pitiful little calves. Was it this Tim of the letter? She couldn't remember. It happened a long time ago and she had tried to forget things after Isaac's death, not remember them.

Isaac died of a heart attack while seated on the toilet. Just like Elvis. From too many packs of Marlboro cigarettes and too many jelly donuts. And too much anger maybe too. She would never forget the sound of his body falling that day. Or the feeling of freedom that settled in after the mourning ended.

One morning a week or so after she found the letter, it came to her. She remembered who Tim was. Yes, she remembered. He was that shy boy about twenty years old with the unruly shock of pale blond hair and the pale too white skin and blue blue eyes who was working there the fall and winter of the dying calves. Tim Something from up around Miles City. He never failed to thank her for the meals she fed him.

He said he was saving up money to move to California or Hawaii, somewhere warm where he could learn to surf. She had teased him about already having the blond good looks, all he lacked was a nice tan. That was Tim, who had been on those long trips to Wisconsin for the poor dying calves.

A couple of weeks later, she showed the letter to Paul, who read it quickly and handed it back to her as though it was hot. "Oh, my god, Mom, where did you get this? What does it mean? Who wrote it?"

"I found it in that old box of your grandmother's. Your dad wrote it."

"But it's a love letter. Dad wrote it? Who's this Tim?"

So she told him.

"So he was gay? Dad was gay?" He started to laugh and she joined in.

"He never sent the letter, so maybe nothing ever happened," Ada said. "Back then, they killed gay boys around here, so maybe his fear kept it from happening." And that would sure explain his intense need to find a wife. Like it meant life and death she thought. It might well have meant just that. "Except on those trips to Wisconsin," she added. "Maybe."

Paul was quiet for a bit. "Wow, that's sad," he said.

Not just for him, Ada thought. "Yes, it is. It's tragic."

"And maybe why he was so damn mean and unhappy."

"Maybe."

"Couldn't you have just thrown that letter away?" Paul asked. "Why drag it out to show me? I don't want to know this shit. And are you seriously going to show it to Amanda?"

"Don't you think I should? It explains a lot. She's entitled to know who her father was. She loved him. The truth will set you free."

"She'll hate you more for it," he predicted.

"She already hates me and I think it might heal those old wounds," Ada said. "That's all I want, peace in the family. And truth."

"Are we talking about the same Amanda?" her son asked. "My sister who still refers to her fifty-year-old self as Daddy's little girl, the one with the shrine in her backyard to her dead father? That one? The one who hates you for living while he died?"

"And for falling in love with one of his young men?" Ada asked. "I think this could fix it."

"I wouldn't," Paul advised. "Amanda is not a fan of the truth."

Amanda had married a man whose mother was from Mexico and his father was a German whose more prosperous wheat farm was north of theirs. Her husband built a small shrine of bricks in their backyard with a plaster Virgin of Guadalupe to watch over the glass box in which her beloved father's ashes rested. She was adamantly opposed to her Mother's plan to scatter the ashes over the farm. She still referred to herself as Daddy's little princess, his pet name for her. Amanda had always been exempt from Isaac's occasional physical abuse and his constant verbal abuse.

The first Sunday of every month was Amanda's day to visit her mother and brother at the old farm. Ada knew it was her odd sense of family duty, not love or caring that fostered these visits which nearly always ended in discord if not another outright fit. Amanda told Paul she wished it had been her mother who died. She had been demanding her fair share of the farm every visit since her dad died.

"It's still Mom's," Paul would tell her. "When you can speak rationally about it, we can discuss me buying it from Mom and then we can talk about your share. In the meantime, it's still Mom's."

Amanda would flounce off in a huff every first Sunday, never pretending she wasn't waiting for Ada's death, asking her time after time if her mother had a will and what was in it. She never missed an opportunity to tell both Paul and her mother that she didn't trust them to do the right thing for her, that they would most likely cheat her out of her inheritance now that her father was gone and there was no one to do the right thing.

"Like the greedy vulture she is," Paul would mutter.

A couple of years ago, after about eight years of Amanda's fits and demands, Ada decided to sell the place to Paul. Paul drove her into Belle Fourche one nice summer day to see her lawyer, who drew up the papers, selling the place to Paul at close to market value.

Paul told Amanda and gave her a paper with the amount of her share and his plan to give her a certain amount each month. She threw the biggest fit of her life, screaming, "Dad would kill you both for this!"

"If he wasn't dead," Ada said under her breath. "Paul can handle these payments to you and it's my land and my decision. And it's a fair price." Neither she nor Paul mentioned that Ada had not asked Paul to pay her for the place. She had enough money to live on and he always helped her in any way he could.

Amanda hired an expensive attorney of her own who told her the same thing her mother and Paul had said. The contract was valid and the price was fair and there was nothing she could do. Her anger and hatred escalated.

Amanda missed a year of Sunday visits in her rage. When her guilt or duty kicked in again, those Sundays became her payday. She demanded her check with every visit. She always made these trips alone; her husband and kids had heard too many awful stories about the bad grandma and thieving brother to want to come with her. They wanted no part of the family war and Amanda scared them.

It was early September, that golden time on the northern plains when another first Sunday rolled around. Ada cleaned her little house thoroughly and laid the letter on the little marble topped table beside her chair. Amanda hadn't missed one Sunday since they had become her payday.

She drove up to the house that Sunday in her new BMW. She waved at Paul who was in the yard watering his new little Chinese elm trees.

Paul watched her as she headed toward the old bunkhouse, now painted a lovely pale yellow, his mom's favorite color. Ada had planted sunflowers down the walkway Paul had made of some local flat pale sandstone rocks. He shut the hose off and followed his sister.

Ada met them at the door. "So nice to see you, Amanda. Come in. I have lemonade."

Paul handed Amanda her usual Sunday check, noting that she carried a new purse, Louis Vuitton it boasted. Amanda loved designer labels and had no taste. The purse was too big for her small frame and an ugly baby poop color with some awkward designs scattered on it here and there.

Ada poured three glasses of lemonade for them and sat back down.

"So, what's up, Mom?" Amanda asked as she plopped down on the couch after grabbing a glass of lemonade. "The new place looks good. Paul outdid himself giving you what you want," she said with a sneer.

"I do like it," Ada said. "And Paul's family needed more room. It's good to have my own place." She picked up the letter and handed it to her daughter.

"What's this?" Amanda asked. She unfolded the paper and read it. "What is this?

Where did you get it? It's Dad's handwriting. I'd know it anywhere. Why do you have this? And who is Tim?"

"One of those young men your father was always hiring," Ada said. "I remember him."

"One you didn't get to first?" Amanda asked.

"Shut up, Amanda," Paul said quietly.

"You did this!" Amanda shrieked at her mother. "You can't quit giving Dad shit even when he's dead, can you?" She got up and started pacing the floor as she reread the letter.

"I thought you should know. It tells you that he did love someone," Ada said.

"He loved me!" Amanda shouted. "Nobody ever loved you! That's why you're doing this." She plopped back down on the couch and began to cry noisily.

"Stop it, Amanda," Paul said.

"And you shut up, Paul, you mealy mouthed thief. You helped her cheat me out of my rightful share of the ranch with that sleazy lawyer's help." She stood up, grabbed her fancy new purse and started to run off as she usually did after anyone tried to talk to her during one of her screaming fits. She put the strap of the purse on her shoulder, then took it off, stopped and turned around, reached inside the big purse and pulled out the pistol her husband had bought for her after a break-in at their house. "I hate you," she screamed. "I've always hated you! And now you're still trying to hurt Dad!"

She aimed the gun at her mother and pulled the trigger.

Paul screamed and ran toward his sister, knocking her down. She dropped the gun and he kicked it away from her and went to his mother. Blood was pouring from her chest. She reached up to touch his face. The light in the room seemed to be fading and she could hear someone screaming. Paul. It was Paul. She closed her eyes and when she opened them again after what seemed like hours later, there was more light and there he was, her old lover, the young man she had fallen in love with because he was kind to her all those years ago. He was young and beautiful again and no longer dead. He held his arms out to her and she flew to him. Paul noted the smile on her face.

"You've killed Mom," he shrieked at his sister.

"I'm sorry! I'm sorry. It was an accident." She was backing up, getting ready to run like the coward she was.

"I was here," Paul said savagely in a tone she had never heard before. "It was no accident. You'll be in prison. How will you spend your money then?" He gently laid his mother back in her chair and walked toward Amanda who had picked up her gun. He jerked it out of her hand and unloaded it while she cried and screamed.

"It was an accident!" Amanda said savagely. She ran for the door and he grabbed her arm and pushed her onto the couch and held her there while he dialed the county sheriff on his cell phone as Amanda screamed no no no. "You know it was an accident!"

"It's over," Paul said as his mother slumped to the floor with that peaceful smile still on her face while her blood ran into the pretty new wool rug.

VERN AND THE END OF THE WORLD
Part One

I'm waiting for my lawyer. It's late January here in Phoenix and it's chilly in this cell. There's no heat turned on yet. Wait for August, one smart ass young deputy told me with a sneer. I wonder if I'll still be here in August.

My lawyer's name is Adam Waymond and he was Vern's lawyer first and now mine. Even though I never took Vern's advice and seldom did what he wanted after I finally got to know him, now I'm calling his lawyer. Maybe it's an attempt to placate Vern, although that is unlikely and unlike me. Or maybe it's just apathy. God knows Vern's biggest complaint about me was my apathy. I guess now he's thinking that over. The last time he saw me, I sure wasn't apathetic.

I decided to write about that last time I saw Vern so that maybe my son, Vern's son, might understand.

Vern and I met when I was eighteen and had just enrolled in Phoenix Community College. My plan even then was to become a teacher. I admit I was an idiot back then when I was eighteen or I would never have been with Vern.

Joyce Keveren

I had never been anywhere or done anything other than what my religious family okayed. Vern was twenty-one and from another world. Boy was I right about that. I had no idea.

He was working at a gas station. That was where I met him, filling up so I could get to my classes. He flirted with me and flattered me and I was susceptible to that. Gradually he bullied me into sex and I was soon pregnant. It was 1965 and the only options my family granted were marriage or death so we got married. Like I said, I was an idiot.

And Vern was right. It wasn't apathy back then, but there was no fire either, no passion. I would learn of passion at a later time with another man who would never accuse me of apathy.

Noah was about three when I got my first teaching job. Yes, he named our son Noah.

"You're going to teach him carpentry, aren't you? So he can build an ark? Right?" I asked.

"You are incredibly underinformed of Biblical things," he informed me. "For the daughter of some religious lunatics especially. God promised no more floods, Eve. Fire. It's fire next time."

I could never understand why that seemed to please him so much.

Vern found a house over on 35th Avenue he insisted we buy because it had a full basement which was rare in Phoenix because of the layer of hard caliche. By we, he meant me because I was the one with a steady income while he did odd jobs and prepared for the nuclear winter to come.

He had become obsessed with thoughts of a nuclear war. He spent most of his time preparing for the end of the world while I took care of the necessary details of daily survival. I was getting good at it.

He subscribed to every magazine and publication he could find about bomb shelters and nuclear fallout and other doomsday problems. He redid one room in the basement to make a nuclear fallout shelter and stocked it with canned goods and bottled water, sleeping bags and blankets, cooking and eating utensils and extra clothing for the three of us. He rarely worked and insisted my salary was enough to keep us going.

"It's not money that will get us through the last days, Eve, it's my knowledge and planning. He grinned a sheepish grin. "Oh, and God too."

His fanatical religious fervor was beginning to eclipse his practical survival concerns. I was beginning to not like him too much but that family religious training he spoke of kicked in and kept me yoked to him, although with more and more unwillingness.

"Those who resist the restraints of the Lord shall perish in their obstinate willfulness." I could hear those words of my paternal grandfather, the fervent Baptist minister, ringing in my ears. My family all called me obstinate back then so much that it should have been my name.

Vern was angry a lot in those early days through the 70's, when Noah was small. He resented having to care for Noah while I was at work even though he had quit working anywhere after I got my teaching degree and I think his anger was also because everyone in America seemed to be having a great time of it, what with the drug culture and the free love while he spent all his time reading survival manuals and the Book of Revelation and he was scaring himself into a frenzy too, with his ear always cocked to detect the first notes from Gabriel's trumpet.

He had fallen in with some church group, The Christian Rebel Angels of Zion Empire or CRAZE. The crazies is what I called them, but their fears and their belief in the last days and the Rapture fit right into that little pocket of insanity he had been clearing in his own head.

I refused to go to any of their meetings after that first one that left me wanting to both laugh and scream. Their beliefs made my God-fearing family look like sane folks.

Vern was pissed about that too, calling me a demon-loving whore. Whore, yes, I admit it, what with that other man, but demon-lover, no way. I didn't even love him and he was the closest thing to a demon I knew. Not whore either, since I had never rented or sold myself. It occurs to me that Vern never knew me at all. He didn't want to either since that would have cut into his ME time.

He let his hair and beard grow and began to look like a crazed prophet who lived off grubs in the desert with his rifle over his shoulder most of the time.

He actually did go off into the Sonoran Desert from time to time to live off the land for a week or two at a time. He never staged these trips in the heat of summer; he wasn't that crazy yet. Once or twice, I caught myself fantasizing about a rabid coyote or a herd of javelinas tearing into him out there in the desert, but prudently kept it to myself.

When he dragged in after a couple of weeks, ten pounds lighter, I dutifully cooked him a steak and ran a bath for him.

He had amassed an arsenal of weapons too; guns of all kinds, a 9mm Barretta handgun like the police use, an old Colt .45, rifles, shotguns, a 50 caliber machine gun the military used, a little 22 pistol, a 30 ought 6 shot gun, a 30 ought lever action rifle, an AK47, an Uzi, 22, 243 and 270 caliber rifles, a 38 special and a little 25 for me, and some others I couldn't identify, along with all the ammunition, enough for a revolution in some small nation. He also had all sorts of knives and even grenades which he stored in the shelter he had built and most of which he had bought with my money.

It all looked pretty official to me and made me think he was prepared for any catastrophe that happened along, all except the chemical toilet which he tried out which left a bit to be desired.

The years went by and I kept on teaching and Noah grew up. The internet came along and aided and abetted his end of the world insanity, making it easier for him to find all the other people who thought like he did. Or didn't think much at all as the case may be.

By 1990, I had put in twenty years teaching. I planned to retire in '95 when I was nearing fifty, but Vern thought different. In his frenzy of preparations for Y2K, he determined he needed a better underground bunker/bomb shelter. He found a piece of land up north of the city in the pine forest near Payson where he could build.

"How much savings do you have?" he demanded. "How much in IRAs?"

I told him. I knew it was useless to not tell him as he would threaten me with not only death from the end of the world thing, but with his usual tactic of twisting my teacher's right arm until I cried or it broke or until I did what he wanted.

"I need that money," he yelled. "We need it if we're going to survive. It's life and death and do you really think those IRAs and CDs will save you?"

He was screaming. "Read Revelation 3:16, Eve." He went to the bookcase and got the Bible. "Revelation 3:16," he yelled. He found the passage and began to read it to me, yelling in my face, "So then, because thou art lukewarm and neither cold nor hot, I will spew ye out of my mouth---that's you, Eve, apathetic! Read it, Eve, you will be spewed out!"

I had a mental vision of a huge person, something like Michelangelo's God figure spewing me out in a shower of saliva as I thought, not hot, Vern? Oh, ye of little faith, Vern. You have no idea how hot I can get. But I wouldn't betray myself and my lover. Not to Vern and the Crazies anyway.

"Calm down, Vern," I said. I watched the vein in his head throbbing and pulsing like it might explode. I imagined it exploding. I almost said you don't want to have a heart attack and miss the end do you? But I wisely kept it to myself.

He lunged toward me anyway, but I evaded him and ran to the front door. He pinned me against the door and his face was so close, I could see the little network of veins in the whites of his eyes. "It's life and death," he hissed. "What do you choose?"

Actually death was starting to look pretty good, but I chose not to tell him that.

So, once again, I knuckled under and he got his piece of land up north and began construction on his upgraded Y2K shelter/temple/survival chamber/love nest. By then, I suspected that he had a thing going with one of the Crazies, a woman named Madeline. He referred to her as Maddie with an odd inflection in his voice, the sound the Crazies made when speaking of God or the Devil who they seemed to worship too.

I started calling her Nutty in my own mind, but once when I said it aloud to him, his eyes narrowed and he started to do his Incredible Hulk transformation so I stopped.

By then, I was heart deep into my own love affair with the man who taught me about passion and I lived mainly to see him and didn't care whether the world ended or not as long as we were together. And I was pretty sure that the turn of the century which was based on arbitrary time keeping, would have little effect other than the meaningless foolishness of a few nutcases like Vern and the Crazies.

When January 1, 2000 rolled around and nothing happened other than the usual dropping of the ball in Times Square and some great fireworks from around the world and the usual gunshots outside my window, Vern finally wandered down to Phoenix from his underground haven, his beard ragged and his eyes wild. He'd been holed up in that dismal bunker for weeks, eating from his canned stores and hadn't bathed much. He was a mess and he was angry.

"Don't be so sad and angry, Vern," I told him. "It's not the end of the world." He didn't think that was funny.

I thought he was going to explode, so I went out to feed the dog and yelled at Noah to come inside. Noah was six foot two now and he worked out.

Vern slunk off to take a shower and lick his wounds, and in a few days wandered back to his underground bunker and Nutty.

I filed for divorce and my lawyer mailed the papers to Vern's lawyer, who tried to get everything he could from me. Instead of selling the house which he demanded, I gave up the rest of my IRAs and savings. My lawyer explained how he had already taken most of his share of my savings to build his bunker up north, so essentially he had a house I had paid for already, such as it was.

I was Vern-free or so I thought. I was broke too, but I still had my home and my job and Noah and my lover. In other words, I had everything I needed and wanted. But Vern still didn't have what he wanted. I should have known.

He was now obsessing about the Mayan prophecies and the end of the Mayan calendar which was winter solstice, December 21, 2012. It was now 2005 and Vern needed to be prepared. He called me to tell me the Christian Rebel Angels of Zion Empire had bought 100 acres up near Strawberry in the forest of northern Arizona. They had already built a huge underground complex that would house their whole flock.

"It's ingenious, Eve," he said. "It's built with a round central area where all the provisions are stockpiled and radiating out around this central area are spokes with individual living areas for family groups. You and I and Noah are family. We need to be there."

"What about Nutty?" I asked. He was a long way away so I was brave.

He sputtered something that was mostly unintelligible, but then he took a breath and controlled himself.

"I need you and Noah here," he growled.

"No, Vern. Never," I told him. "We're divorced. There is no we. Did you forget?"

"I want to move there, Eve." He was whining like a little boy now.

"Well, go ahead, Vern, with my blessing for you and your girlfriend." I hung up but he called again six months later, still pleading and whining. If he had been talking in person to me, the whining would have changed to something more aggressive, like hitting me. Or twisting my arm. That thought made me angry.

"If you think it's the end of the world and the Rapture, why do you need a communal bunker? Can't you just wait to be taken up into the heavens with all the other pure ones while us sinners writhe in agony down here on earth? Don't you want to be where you can see that?"

I could tell he was enraged, but he attempted to control himself. That's when I knew he wanted something and he would not give up. "What do you want, Vern?" I asked. "What now?"

"I want our family to be together, Eve. That's all."

"Forget it, Vern." I hung up.

Of course, that wasn't the end of it. He started bombarding me with e-mails, imploring, begging, persuading, then threatening.

I shut down my e-mail account and opened a new one. I got caller ID and didn't answer his calls. I thought about a restraining order, but rejected that idea because he was a hundred miles away in his home sweet bunker with his CRAZE woman. What could he possibly want from me? He already had all my money.

A couple of years later, two years closer to the end of the Mayan calendar, I found out. The CRAZE people needed $100,000 to add on to their underground city so Vern and Nutty could move in there. Nutty must not have a dime.

He sent a certified letter to me telling me this: He wanted me to sell the house, my home which I had paid for with no help from him so he could move into the Crazie's complex.

Joyce Keveren

His cell phone number was on the letter. I dialed the number and when I heard him answer, I said, "Never, Vern, never. I am not your wife. I pretty much hate you and never want to see your face again. You have gotten all you ever will from me. The world is not going to end anytime soon so just kill yourself." I hung up and thought the problem was solved. I owed him nothing.

On winter solstice, December 21, 2011, one year before the Mayan calendar ran out, he paid me a visit.

He had to knock as the locks had been changed since he had lived there. I opened the door and he shoved me aside and came in. He was holding one of his many guns, a small handgun, maybe the little 25 he had bought for me.

"It's loaded, Eve. I've called a realtor who will be here tomorrow. You will sell the house and you will give me the money. It's for our family."

I thought back to a time during our divorce when he had put a piece of paper and a pen in front of me and twisted my arm until I wrote a note saying that all we owned was his and not mine, that it would all go to him in the divorce.

He's like a goddamn bulldog, never gives up, never lets go.

I walked slowly over to the couch and sat down. "Tomorrow, Vern. I can do it tomorrow. Does that mean you will spend the night here?"

He nodded like he had just thought of it.

"Put the gun away and I'll fix us something to eat." I walked toward the kitchen. He followed me. The gun was still in his hand. I put a frozen dinner in the microwave as he watched.

"So you still can't cook," he sneered.

I felt a flash of hatred take over my brain, but I forced myself to smile at him. The bastard has a gun, I told myself. Calm down.

My purse with the keys to my car was on the big Mexican plate on the table by the front door. I decided to make a run for it after I got him seated at the table over his Swedish meatballs. I made a pot of coffee and placed two plates and silverware on the kitchen table and put another tray in the microwave.

"Make yourself comfortable, Vern," I said as I headed for the front door. "I'll go to the little store and get some dessert," I called to him as I walked quickly to the front door. I grabbed my purse and was out the door and into the car just as he ran out behind me, that gun still in his hand.

"Oh, no, you don't," he screamed as I drove off. Then I heard some pinging sounds on the back of the car. That bastard was shooting at me. I kept driving. I could see him in the rear-view mirror under the light by the front door, his face distorted by rage, the gun still in his hand. I thought irrationally that I had paid for that goddamn gun he was trying to kill me with and the thought enraged me. My house was in a cul-de-sac with high fences on both sides between me and the neighbors who evidently weren't home as there were no lights on in either of the two houses next to mine.

I made a decision then and turned that 2006 Impala around like the antelope it was named for and drove back up to the house at maybe fifty miles an hour.

Vern was standing under the car port at the entrance to the bomb shelter where he had built a solid block wall on one side of the utility room. He had filled that wall with cement, I guess, just in case he wanted a place to look out the window at the devastation of the nuclear winter.

All I could think was the bastard had shot at me. With one of the goddamn guns I had bought for the worthless, unemployed dumbass nutcase. He shot at me! I saw a field of red in front of me, like the cape the bull sees in the bullring.

I gunned the Impala and just as he raised that 360 or 25 or whatever the hell it was to take another shot, I ran the car smack dab into him.

I pretty much had forgotten that wall was solid cement. It didn't give. I heard some odd sounds, a thud when the car hit his body and his body hit that wall, a screech of metal when the fenders bent and the screech of the brakes when I finally hit them and a yelp from Vern.

I backed up and drove down the block to the little store, our neighborhood market whose name was Happy Market where I ran inside and asked my friend Malik who owned the store to call 911 to report an accident.

"We need an ambulance," I said.

"What happened? Are you all right?" he asked.

"I ran into Vern," I said.

When he put the phone down, he asked, "What do you mean you ran into him? Like at the mall or what?"

"No, no. I mean I ran into him. With the car," I said.

"Oh, shit," Malik said. "Well, the ambulance is on the way."

I waited for the police and the ambulance in the Impala outside the store. I didn't go home because I was still afraid of Vern, although I didn't need to be right then.

I went back to the house when I saw the police drive by. Vern was laying on the ground with the pistol a few feet away. His legs were all crooked and looked broken. I heard the ambulance coming down the street.

"He was shooting at me," I told the policeman who had picked up the gun and unloaded it.

"She ran into me," Vern moaned.

The policeman and paramedics got Vern loaded into the ambulance and then the policeman turned to me and asked, "Did you run over him?"

"Not exactly over him. Into him," I admitted. "He was shooting at me. Look at the bullet holes in the car."

"They're in the back of the car like you were driving away from him," he said as he checked the damage to the front end.

"I was, but I turned around and came back. To run over—I mean, to run into him. I didn't really plan it. I just did it."

The policeman gave me a look much like the looks I used to give the Crazies, put me into the back of his car and took me straight to the Fourth Avenue Jail where I am now. Again.

It turned out Vern didn't die of his many injuries, but it took months for all the broken arms and legs and ribs to heal and the internal injuries were pretty awful too.

Noah said he's limping around up there at the CRAZE place and he and Maddie are almost moved in now. They are only waiting for their lawsuit against me to be settled so the house can be sold, so they can buy their $100,000 piece of bunker which they compare to Elijah's fiery chariot and horses even though it's a wheel, The Wheel in the Sky, they are calling it, even though it is obviously in the ground. They think that whole goddamn unwieldy concrete mess of canned and dried foods, bottled water, bibles, Pampers, Depends and chemical toilets and crazed end of the world people that I accidentally helped pay for, God forgive me, will rise like magic into the air and take them to heaven just like Elijah.

And Noah said Vern gave God the credit. God had answered his prayers for the $100,000 he and Nutty needed. I don't think so, Vern. No, I don't. There is no God anywhere who would break almost every bone in your body to fulfill your idiotic desires. No, Vern, it was me and I'm paying my dues for it too because the State of Arizona agrees with me too. God had nothing to do with it.

I will be out of here in another month or so, then I have to serve another two years in a women's prison of their choice and then I'll be free.

The sentence was light as my lawyer, Adam, who used to be Vern's lawyer, explained. "Attempted murder gets a much longer sentence," he said.

"I wasn't attempting to murder him," I said for perhaps the 114th time.

"What were you attempting?" he asked. He didn't ask me that on the witness stand. He was afraid of what I would say. He often called me a loose cannon. I got used to it because he was trying to help me. And it was so much better than 'apathetic whore' or Vern's latest, Frigid Bitch, although it has a nice ring to it and reminds me of the poetry of Eminem that I like so much. Frigid Bitch, I loathe you and so on. I should work on that. I will have time when I am sentenced. In the meantime, I am trying to do what the counselor here told me to do, distance myself from Vern, be detached, try not to react to him or overreact emotionally.

"Like run into him with a car?" I asked.

"Exactly," she said. She also encouraged me to write while I'm in jail too.

It turned out to be a plus that Adam was Vern's lawyer before he was mine because that meant he knew Vern and could easily understand why someone might want to ram him into a cement wall with an

Impala and he could convey that to a jury at just the right time with just the right words.

"So what were you attempting, Eve?" he asked me again.

"Two things," I said. "I have thought about this a lot. One, I was trying to get him to stop shooting at me. I was trying to knock the gun out of his hand."

"Well, you did that. And two?"

"I was trying to get him to leave without taking my house and the $100,000 he wanted.

That didn't quite work. He got my house and his $100,000 and his heart's desire to live in the Crazies' fancy bunker. But he sure did leave. And it's only six months now until the end of the Mayan calendar."

Adam grinned. I grinned back. I knew he liked me which was a bit surprising since he knew what I had done. My old lover, who was not so tolerant, or so brave, had escaped. I guess he really was afraid of me. But Adam wasn't afraid.

"Do you think Vern and all those other CRAZE people will get their heart's desire?"

"The end of the world?" I asked. "Not a chance."

"So you won," he said as he prepared to leave me in my 6 by 8 cell with the open toilet, my only home now. For a while.

"I won," I agreed. "Vern's gone. But you're not. And I'm okay with my sentence. I deserve it. You just can't go around trying to disarm a lunatic with a car. I've learned my lesson. Probably I won't do it again. What are the chances I would be stupid enough to get involved with a vicious nutcase like Vern again? So thank you, Adam."

"Adam and Eve," he said with that grin I liked. "I like the sound of that. Those two had a whole new world as I remember. I'll be here when you get out. Unless the world does end."

"Not a chance," I said into his ear. "Not now when I'm free. Vern free, that is."

VERN AND THE END OF THE WORLD
Part Two
LAILA'S STORY

I met Laila when she was sent to the same women's minimum-security prison I was sent to.

She was assigned to work in the prison library with me as soon as the warden learned she was a college graduate and spoke several languages.

I liked her the moment I met her. She was not only beautiful but kind as well, a quality I now think is the most important for happiness and she was smart too.

I also value sanity after spending all those years with Vern, whose obsession with the End of the World made him as unbalanced as a washing machine full of tennis shoes.

Gradually through the months we worked together cleaning, dusting, organizing and cataloging the donated books, checking them out to the prisoners and keeping records, I learned Laila's story. It was a comedy of errors, or would have been if she hadn't landed in this prison.

Joyce Keveren

Laila was born into an affluent Iraqi family. Her father was a well-known doctor in Baghdad where the family lived in a three-story house in a good neighborhood.

She had one older brother, Abdullah whose name she told me means Servant of Allah.

"What does Laila mean?" I asked.

"Night Beauty," she said, blushing.

"That's very appropriate for you."

So we exchanged stories. I told her about my misadventures with Vern and how I got here by hitting him with my car. "What happened to you that you landed in here?" I asked her.

"So very many things. I must start at the beginning so you will understand."

She told me that in 2003, when the Americans invaded Iraq in that grandiose and arrogant mistake, Shock and Awe, her father was still practicing medicine. His office was on the bottom floor of their house and he worked long hours, often for little or nothing because that is what the people had after all the Shock and Awe bombings, little or nothing.

He treated the many injuries from the bombings as well as the everyday illnesses of the people, many of whom had lost homes and possessions, jobs, arms and legs and means of survival.

"He was a good, kind man," Laila said. "He had a reputation as an honest man who would pay his debts on time even when his patients couldn't pay him. Like your Abraham Lincoln. I admire him too and my father was murdered just like Lincoln was too."

"I'm so sorry. It must have been terrible for you."

"It was. For all of us, my mom and my brother and me."

"That happens a lot," I told her. "People who speak out for peace and equality often get killed. JFK, Bobby Kennedy, Martin Luther King, Jesus."

"John Lennon," she added. Gandhi, Benazir Bhutto. All heroes of mine."

"Tell me about it," I said. "If you want to."

"My father treated the American soldiers he found who were wounded too. The rebels, al-Qaeda and other groups labeled him a traitor for these acts of kindness and he died when his car was bombed. My mother was ill that day and didn't go with him to buy food for the house or she would have died too.

"After we buried him, Abdullah, my mother and I contacted a cousin of my mother's in Phoenix and because we still had some money my mother had hidden, we made our way to America before we were killed too. We flew from Baghdad to Istanbul and then on the New York. From there we flew to Phoenix.

"That helped us greatly. We stayed with my mother's cousin until we were able to buy a small, modest house in west Phoenix after Abdullah and I found jobs. I also went to college.

"Later, Abdullah got involved with a group of young al Qaeda sympathizers and he went to Yemen to be trained. Our mother cried bitterly, trying to dissuade him but he wouldn't be budged. She asked him if he had forgotten who it was that had killed our father. Abdullah would not listen. He said our father was a traitor to help the enemy and what he was doing was the right thing to do, that our father was wrong and that he was responsible for his own death. He embraced al Qaeda's programs. He believed he had started to live up to his name, servant of Allah.

"My mother and I, who were happy with the freedom for women we found in America, were alarmed and frightened for him. My mother, even though she was devoutly religious, believed taking the path of violence was wrong and that it would lead to his destruction.

"I had been studying religions at school and I learned of Mahatma Gandhi who I loved and admired for his peacefulness and his brilliance. He had been an attorney and I was planning to do that too. I wanted to help the women of my country and other countries of the Middle East to become free. Benazir Bhutto was also my role model. She stood up for the rights of women in her country of Pakistan, knowing they would kill her. She had courage like Gandhi. We have to make the changes peacefully. Like Gandhi. Abdullah was wrong."

"I think you're right," I told her. "Peace is the right way. But Abdullah was programmed."

Laila looked up at me through the shelf of books she was dusting. She smiled. "Yet I hear that you are in here for running over your husband with a car."

"My ex-husband. I ran INTO him with a car, not over him and yes, that's true. I don't ever want to do anything like that again even though he sort of had it coming. And I hear you tried to rob a bank." I smiled back at her.

"They say that," she agreed. "I think even my lawyer believed it."

"It's not true?"

She shook her head. Another inmate came into the library so our discussion ended for that day.

In the next few days, she told me more of what happened that brought her to this prison.

"Sometimes just to please my mother, who was so sad and scared for Abdullah who was, by this time on the lists of the FBI and CIA and Homeland Security as a possible terrorist, I would wear the abaya, the women's dress of Iraq that covered me from my neck down to the floor. I still had a couple of them, both black the traditional color. I prefer American clothes, especially in the Phoenix summer, but Mama is old and traditional."

"And brainwashed," I added, before I thought.

"That too," Laila agreed, "I will never make my daughter wear that."

"You have a daughter?"

"I do. She's three now."

"Where is she?"

"With her father and grandmother in Mazatlán, Mexico."

"Could they come here?" I asked.

"It would be hard now."

"Yes, it would," I agreed. "With all the flapdoodle about immigration and illegal aliens. It's a mess. It's shameful. The melting pot of the world is now boiling over and spitting out. And we're all from somewhere else. We all should be free to go anywhere we want, whenever we want."

"We would be dead if we hadn't been allowed to come here," Laila said.

"I have a son," I told her. "He's in college now. His name is Noah."

"Good name. My little girl's name is Laila Elena. Her father named her."

"I know you miss her."

She started to cry softly. "Every moment," she said.

Laila continued to tell me her story as the days went by and we worked together. One day she said she wore her black abaya with a flowered headscarf that covered her forehead and hair, and under the abaya, she wore a white cotton summer dress with spaghetti straps because the abaya was itchy. Her mother had frowned to see her in the white dress with bare shoulders and her long legs bare.

"I wore the abaya because it pleased my mother. Mama was grieving so over Abdullah that day. I couldn't add to her troubles." She sighed. "Big mistake. I went to my bank that day to withdraw some money. I had so admired Gandhi that I had begun his practice of not speaking on Mondays. I also prayed a lot to Allah and sometimes to Jesus and I tried to follow the Eightfold path of the Buddha and I did the prayers of Islam facing toward Mecca. And I entreated the Divine Mother of the Hindus. I took bits and pieces from everywhere into my own private spirit life."

"I do that too," I told her. "Probably not as well as you do though."

She smiled at me, a lovely, accepting smile that held so much sadness I could barely look at her.

"So I wrote out a withdrawal slip and a note for the teller at the bank that said Hello I want to withdraw some funds. Thank you for your help. When I got to the window, I saw it was a new girl. She was very young. I smiled and handed her the note through the little slot in all that bulletproof glass thing they had installed after a couple of robberies. There was also an armed guard on duty. That girl took one look at me in my abaya and that note and she overreacted like she was on TV or drugs and she screamed something about a robbery. I looked around to see what she was talking about and realized it was me she was screaming about so I grabbed my note and withdrawal slip and took another look around to see the guard who was by the front door pull out his gun and I ran out the side door which was close so that was lucky and I was wearing flat shoes and I am a fast runner.

"I heard a bullet whiz by my head as I went through the door. Lucky that guard was overweight—fat really and slow. I ran around the corner of the bank building and into a six-foot tall, tangled old stand of oleander. I worked my way into it and became very still. My face and hands were all scratched up. I could see the guard looking this way and that, shaking his head and putting his gun away. He left and must have gone back inside and called the police, because soon I heard sirens. I stayed where I was next to the cement wall hidden in those scratchy, poisonous oleanders until the two police cars left. Then I made my way all the way through that hedge and came out several hundred feet from the bank building. I was all scratched up and my hands were bleeding a bit.

"The doctor's office my mother and I went to was right there, only a few feet away. I walked quickly around the end of the building into the office and went to the ladies' restroom, where I took the abaya and the scarf off. I shook my hair out. It was long and curly and I tied the scarf around my waist over the white dress, washed my face and hands and combed my hair, put on some makeup to cover the scratches and put on some lipstick. I found a dark plastic bag in the trash and I put the abaya into it and shoved it down into the trash can.

"Then I called home."

"They thought you were trying to rob the bank?" I asked.

"Yes. They still think so. I had kept the note, but as my lawyer pointed out, people would believe I could have written it anytime."

"That silly teller caused the trouble," I said.

"I don't blame her. It was the fear in everyone at that time. And that abaya. It was worse than this ugly orange jumpsuit. Like the burka. Those clothes make prisoners of all the women who are forced to wear them. I have more freedom here in this prison than I would ever have at home in Baghdad wearing that black tent."

"You think so?" I asked. I hate these damn orange jumpsuits."

"Me too. But here I can say that. I would not dare to speak like that at home of the abaya." She gave me a defiant look.

"Here, even here in this prison, I can speak my mind freely to you. On any subject. I can criticize the government and speak to men as an equal. I am free here, even though I am locked up."

She went on to say her cousin who was living with them answered the phone when she called from the doctor's office. He said the police had already been at her home. It was on the afternoon news. She was a hunted woman. She thought it over and decided to run and hide for a while.

"I asked my cousin to take the bus and bring me my small suitcase on wheels with some extra clothes. I told him to have my mom pack it. I told him to ask her to send all the cash money she had laying around along with my passport and some tennis shoes, shirts, pants, a dress or two, a jacket, enough clothes for a couple of weeks or a month maybe. I had no idea it would be almost three years before I returned."

She gave her car keys to her cousin and told him to take her car home but not until after she was gone. Her mother, who always kept a lot of cash around just in case of another emergency, sent her almost $2500. She decided to take a bus to Nogales, AZ.

She was lucky. The only bus of the day headed south for Nogales was leaving almost as soon as she got to the Buckeye Road bus station and the police had not yet stationed anyone there to watch, mistakenly thinking she would head for home. And they were looking for a young woman in an abaya, not an androgynous looking person in a pair of shorts and a t-shirt and a ball cap with a picture of the Statue of Liberty on it.

It was almost dark when the bus pulled out and headed south for the border.

"Have you watched a lot of old Western movies?" I asked her.

She grinned and nodded.

"That's a tradition of the old West, to run for the border when you're in trouble with the law."

"That's probably where I got the idea."

"It never occurred to me," I told her, "when I was in big trouble."

"You didn't have a brother on the FBI list either," she pointed out.

"That's true and also the police had me in custody before I could run. Because I called them," I added.

"I had my citizenship papers but I was afraid. Back home in Iraq, I would already be dead, I think. For dishonoring the family. Actually, I did that when I went out with my last boyfriend."

"I can relate to that," I told her. "So what happened when you got to Nogales?"

"When I got to Nogales, Arizona, I got a motel room near the border. I used a made-up name. I went to a drugstore and bought a pair of scissors and some blond hair dye, and a pair of big sunglasses, cut my long hair off and dyed it blond. The next morning, I shoved what hair was left under the ball cap and I walked across the border pretending to be a tourist for a day."

"I got a taxi and asked the driver in Spanish to take me to a nice hotel. I'm good with languages so the driver chatted away in Spanish and I told him I was from the only place whose name I could remember, Guaymas.

"I was so scared and alone. I had stopped calling home, had thrown my cell phone away at the clinic in Phoenix so they couldn't trace that. I was watching the news in Nogales and there were still reports of the Phoenix police searching for the girl bank robber in the abaya whose brother was on the terrorist lists.

"I remembered Abdullah saying how sorry he felt for young American girls who had no family protection, not like the girls at home had. I told him that was maybe true, but at least they weren't killed for making a small mistake like going out with a boy. 'For dishonoring the family,' he yelled at me.

"But now I was alone and really had no protection. I was so frightened."

"You were brave," I said, "and you are setting an example for women everywhere."

"I'm still afraid," she told me, "not brave and I still haven't become a lawyer and gone back to Iraq to help the women there as I wanted to."

"But you will help them by just being you. By telling your story."

She smiled a brave little smile at me and went on with her story. "I spent several days in that hotel hiding out, pretending to be Mexican. It occurred to me that I was now an illegal alien in Mexico. That seemed very funny to me after hearing all the talk of all those bad, evil, thieving, raping illegals sneaking into America and how upset that made some people, like that ugly president. And here I was, a fugitive from the law, sneaking into Mexico.

"I got tired of eating at the same little café at the hotel so I asked a taxi driver to take me to a good restaurant. He thought I was a tourist so he took me to the Cavern, a famous local bar and restaurant in Nogales. It was a real cave that used to be a jail. Geronimo was held there by the Federales. I was wearing my regular uniform now, the shorts and ball cap and I had added a beautiful Mexican blouse with embroidered roses and birds on it. I ordered some chili rellenos and coke and listened to the mariachi band that played there. I liked their music so much that I spent several evenings listening to them play. I loved that happy music. It was the only thing that made me feel better while I stayed in Nogales. It helped me to forget what had happened.

"I was still lonely and scared and afraid to even call home, but I loved those mariachi musicians. The band had five members and one of the guitar players was young and so handsome. He smiled at me and came to my table when they were on a break and we talked in Spanish and I let him think I was a Mexican citizen. He wanted me to come back the next night and I did. I had only had one boyfriend in college but Mama watched me like an eagle and wouldn't let me go out so I was very inexperienced with men. But I liked this one. He looked at me when he sang the love songs with the mariachis and his smile was just for me too. I think I was falling in love with him right there while running from the police.

"He told me his name was Emilio Velasquez and I only said I was Laila and I avoided telling him anything else so I wouldn't have to lie.

"He said he was from Mazatlán and he was only there in Nogales for a short time filling in for his cousin in the mariachi band and he would be leaving for Mazatlán and home where he played at a big resort hotel with his brothers in their own mariachi band.

"I was sad to think of him leaving and he could see that I didn't want him to go.

"I had been in Nogales for almost a month by then. I didn't know what to do, so I bought a burner phone and called home to see if the police had given up their search for me, thinking that was possible and I could tell Emilio the truth. Oh, what a big mistake that was."

"What happened?"

"My mother said there was a policeman there monitoring the phones and they traced the call so they knew where I was. My cousin took the phone and told me to run again. They would soon be after me."

"That night Emilio told me his cousin was back and he would be driving Emilio south to Hermosillo where he would take a plane home to Mazatlán. He said he didn't want to leave me. Without even thinking it over, I said, 'Take me with you.'

"He was surprised, but he had to go back to the bandstand to play some more. When the band stopped playing that night, he came to me and we went to my hotel room and I told him everything. The truth. I was afraid it would scare him and he would run, but what did I have to lose? In any case, I had to run some more. Soon.

"He hugged me and we kissed and he told me to pack my things and I checked out of the hotel and paid the bill while Emilio went to find his cousin.

"I wasn't at all sure he would ever come back, but he did and he brought his cousin. Emilio had taken off his charro suit and now wore Levis. He introduced me to his cousin and they put my suitcase into the pickup and we left Nogales that night. His cousin's name was Enrique and he laughed and kept teasing Emilio about young love and love at first sight. Emilio had decided not to share my whole story, not because he didn't trust Enrique, but just to protect me.

"Enrique drove us that night to Hermosillo and we waited at the airport for the next plane to Mazatlán.

"While we waited, Emilio came up with a plan. He lived next door to his mother in Mazatlán in a little house not far from the beach. His mother was old and very set in her ways. She went to mass two or three times a week and she would never tolerate him bringing girlfriends home.

"His plan was to tell her that I was from a fine family in Nogales and that we were in love and would be married in the church as soon as the priest would do it. 'Are you in love?' I asked him. I was in a strange state of mind from living a sheltered life totally controlled by my parents who would have chosen a husband for me, most likely an older man I had never met, someone they thought suitable. And I would have forever been covered by yards of material, my life planned for me just like my mother's life had been planned for her. I had accepted all that.

"And now here I was, in a strange city, in a foreign land with a handsome young musician I knew little of, hiding out from the law of the United States of America, wearing a little white dress with my legs bare. And my experience with sex was limited to a few furtive kisses with a fellow law student in a dark movie theatre. I was afraid of this handsome boy but I wanted him too and I was more afraid of the FBI and the police who were after me. And of Abdullah too. He had been making noises about how I had dishonored the family.

"What did he say when you asked him if he was in love with you?" I asked.

"He said yes, he was falling like a star on fire. He said he would not lie about that. And so was I. All those love songs he sang to me were working. And he said he wanted to protect me because he believed me when I said I had not tried to rob a bank. I am not that stupid and I didn't need money that bad. He said he had been praying to the Virgin of Guadalupe to send him a beautiful girl to love, not one of the homely daughters of his mother's friends. And she had. So now I had one more person to pray to, along with the Divine Mother, the Virgin of Guadalupe.

"Maybe they're the same," I said. "So what happened?"

"I lived for three months in Emilio's mother's house and she watched me like a hawk, just like my own mother, and she taught me how to make tortillas and tamales and mole and she took me to the old cathedral three times a week and she finally gave us her blessing and Emilio and I got married. I never did know what he told his mother about why none of my family showed up. I didn't want to know.

"I worked as a maid at the hotel where he played for a while, then as the concierge because I knew many languages and Emilio had taught me all of the tourist attractions around Mazatlán.

"I learned to love that city and his mother and most especially Emilio who was good to me. I was so happy except I missed my mother. And even Abdullah. But I was afraid to call. So Emilio asked his cousin Enrique, the mariachi musician from Nogales who visited Phoenix from time to time to play at a club there with his band to take a message to my mom. He did it twice, once when I got married and once when Maria Elena was born. I sent pictures.

"My mother made the mistake of telling Abdullah and showed him the pictures and in his zeal to keep the family honor, he turned me in to the FBI. Anonymously of course."

"Of course, the coward," I muttered. "How's that for honor?"

Laila stopped speaking.

"And they found you," I said.

"Yes, they found me and took me back to Phoenix and I wound up here."

"I'm sorry."

"But if I hadn't worn the abaya that day and if it hadn't been a Monday of Gandhi silence and if the guard hadn't overreacted and thought I was robbing the bank, I would never have met Emilio. Now I live and work on a tropical Pacific beach in a beautiful city. I have a man I love who loves me back and a little girl and a job where I meet people from all over the world and they pay me to talk to them. My life is good. Or was good. If Abdullah doesn't kill me that is."

"Where is he?" I asked.

"I don't know. When the FBI took me back to Phoenix, he was there, hiding out in my mother's house. He was so angry with me, he risked getting arrested.

"I was out on bail, home too, waiting for my lawyer to tell me when the trial would begin.

"And Abdullah was saying things like 'I wish we were home in Baghdad so I could kill you, so I could end this the right way.' He really believed this. His anger and humiliation made him crazy. He said he wanted to strap a bomb to me and sacrifice me to kill some infidels so I wouldn't die as useless as I had lived. I told him to go ahead and kill me now. Right here. Right now. I was calm.

"'You'd like that wouldn't you?' he screamed at me. 'Not too much,' I told him, but he was too full of anger to understand the irony. And I think he was jealous because I had Emilio, someone who loved me." Her eyes were full of tears. "Then in a couple of months, after Abdullah left to protect himself because he wanted to live too, my mother died. She had a heart attack and died in the hospital."

"Oh, honey," I said. I looked into her beautiful dark eyes and saw the endless depth of sorrow there. I put my arms around her there in the library of the women's prison. She stated to cry. She was shaking.

"I killed my mother. I killed her," she mumbled. Abdullah was right to want to kill me. I thought about killing myself."

I held her away from me and looked into her eyes again. "No, he wasn't right and you did not kill anyone. The whole sad mess of all your lives, yours, your mother's, your father's, Abdullah's, that's what killed her. And Abdullah will not kill you when you are released because you will fly right back to Emilio and your little girl and the beaches of Mazatlán where you will be safe."

"But, Eve, he can find me there," she said.

I was still hugging her and she was still crying softly.

"Now listen here," I whispered so the armed guard at the door wouldn't hear. "I will be released before you and when you get out of here, I will drive you to the airport, buy a ticket for Mazatlán. Then when you are in the air safely headed for Emilio and your little girl, I can drive my Impala into Abdullah for you. Remember, I know how to do that."

She smiled and the tears stopped and we both began to laugh.

"Maybe both of us can run into him before I get on the plane," she whispered. "Then you can get on the plane with me so nobody will ever have to come back to this jail."

"That's a good plan. I like that. Maybe I can find a mariachi of my own."

"We're just talking, aren't we?"

"Yes. But it's free. Remember that First Amendment? But I really will buy the ticket and put you on the plane to Mazatlán. We probably won't run my car into Abdullah even though he has earned it. Unless we have to, that is."

www.ingramcontent.com/pod-product-compliance
Lightning Source LLC
LaVergne TN
LVHW091552060526
838200LV00036B/808